With an international reputation a[...] Butlin is one of Scotland's most a[...] up writing fulltime he was, at var[...] band, a barnacle scraper on Thames barges, a footman attending embassies and country houses, and a male model.

His works include the novels *The Sound of My Voice* (winner of the Prix Mille Pages 2004 and Prix Lucioles 2005, both for Best Foreign Novel), *Night Visits* and most recently *Belonging*, two collections of stories, *Vivaldi and the Number 3* (all published by Serpent's Tail) and *The Tilting Room*, as well as six books of poetry. Besides his radio plays, much of his work has been broadcast in Britain and abroad. His fiction and poetry have been translated into over ten languages.

In spring 2007 he received an award from the Thomas Wright Memorial Fund for a two-year Writer's Bursary from the Scottish Arts Council.

He has travelled widely and now lives in Edinburgh with his wife, the writer Regi Claire, and their dog.

Praise for earlier titles from Ron Butlin

The Sound of My Voice

'One of the greatest pieces of fiction to come out of Britain in the '80s...Butlin's book is a stylistic triumph...I anticipate that *The Sound of My Voice* will receive the recognition it deserves as a major novel' Irvine Welsh

'One of the most inventive and daring novels ever to have come out of Scotland. Ron Butlin is that rarest of breeds – a poet who takes the novel form and shows that it is ripe for reinvention. Playful, haunting and moving, this is writing of the highest quality' Ian Rankin

Night Visits

'Beautifully structured…Butlin empathises as well as any writer dealing with the pain of adolescent trauma I've read…What makes the achievement special, however, is the way in which warped adolescent yearning is interwoven with a very different and repressed yearning, that of Malcolm's Aunt Fiona [who is] an archetype of inner corrosion and suffering…Butlin handles the delicate savagery of her condition with a rare combination of sympathy and detachment, and its climax…is as fine in its portrayal of psychological destruction and reconstruction as *The Sound of My Voice*' *Books in Scotland*

'Sick, disturbing, menacing, exceptionally good…Excellently depicted and a credit to the skill and compassion of Butlin, this is contemporary fiction at its classic best' *The Void*

'Butlin's crisp prose oscillates between the real and the surreal, providing the perfect poetic metaphor for this powerful portrait of corrosion and pain' *Glasgow Herald*

'In his dark debut novel, *The Sound of My Voice*, Butlin pulled the reader into a world of twisted longing and inner fantasies among fractured characters. This second novel reaches for the same depths and, as with the best psychological tales, succeeds because it leaves the real terrors to the imagination' *The Scotsman*

'This Bergman-bleak novel is devastating but eventually uplifting. Marvellous' *Uncut*

'Though the setting lends itself to gothic overstatement, Butlin's exploration of emotional abuse is shocking without being sensationalist. As Fiona draws the boy away from his mother into her fantasy world, he is careful never to let repugnance for her as perpetrator outweigh sympathy for her as victim' *Guardian*

Vivaldi and the Number 3

'This collection is an extraordinary read. It is extraordinary in its concept, extraordinary in its delivery, extraordinary in the emotions it manages to evoke…wry, satirical and deeply moving… heart-stoppingly beautiful…[Butlin] is a master' *The New Review*

'Brilliantly conceived…Playing with biography (though never fast and loose) Butlin nips seamlessly in and out of anachronisms, conflating history like a squeezed piano accordion…[he] can take an idea and fly with it to the far reaches of his imagination, developing oblique studies not only of the composers themselves but of their music' *The Herald*

'These stories are hymns to the artistic temperament' *The Times*

'Wickedly funny…witty and contemporary' *Classic FM Magazine*

'Richly surreal stories…an unalloyed triumph…light and yet learned. Gloriously anachronistic…playful, funny and accessible. Wit, humanity and daring…A brilliant and surreal collection of sketches' *Sunday Herald*

'Funny, eloquent, quirky and desperately sad…Everything is mingled in Butlin's world – past and present, dream and waking – with daring and deftness…(A) bubble of lightness (that) somehow carries up with it a heavy stone of sorrow' *Independent on Sunday*

'A deft balance between the comic and the moving…there's a passionate humanity in the stories…compelling…powerful… expressed with a breathtaking clarity and precision…full of hard truth, darkness and light' *The Sandstone Review*

Belonging

'A gripping read – a real page-turner' *Guardian*

'A remarkable book, a seemingly simple tale of wanderlust told in precise, spare prose, yet with a devastating emotional impact to rival much weightier and more-lauded tomes...Butlin expertly bring[s] his landscapes alive with incredible vivacity...a terrible psychological heart of darkness which is as terrifying as it is compelling. Harrowingly honest...this is a truly moving piece of work' *The List*

'Lovers of fast-paced mysteries will find nothing lacking in *Belonging*. It takes the finest features of the suspense novel, and combines them with the 20-something metaphysics of Alan Warner. The result is both mesmerising and serious' *Scotland on Sunday*

'*Belonging* extends and revitalises the traditional Gothic horror tale' *Edinburgh Review*

'The horror invoked in *Belonging* is akin to the nightmares of *The Shining* and *The Towering Inferno*...Butlin creates a tense and acute claustrophobia' *Sunday Herald*

Other works by Ron Butlin

Fiction
The Tilting Room
The Sound of My Voice
Night Visits
Vivaldi and the Number 3
Coming on Strong
Belonging

Poetry
The Wonnerfuu Warld o John Milton
Stretto
Creatures Tamed by Cruelty
The Exquisite Instrument
Ragtime in Unfamiliar Bars
Histories of Desire
Without a Backward Glance: New and Selected Poems

Drama
The Music Box
We've Been Had
Blending In

Opera libretti
Markheim
Dark Kingdom
Faraway Pictures
Good Angel, Bad Angel
The Perfect Woman

no more angels

Stories by Ron Butlin

First published in 2007 by Serpent's Tail,
an imprint of Profile Books Ltd
3a Exmouth House
Pine Street
London ECIR OJH
website: www.serpentstail.com

Designed and typeset at Neuadd Bwll, Llanwrtyd Wells

Printed and bound in Great Britain by Bookmarque Ltd,
Croydon, Surrey

10   9   8   7   6   5   4   3   2   1

These stories are for Ian Baillie, Simon Brown, Helen
Kennedy, Eddie Morgan and, of course, my wife Regi.

Special thanks to all at Serpent's Tail for their support in
bringing out this book. Also to Reuben for the use of his name.

Contents

Acknowledgements

Many of these stories have already been published in successive editions of *New Writing Scotland* or have appeared in the following magazines and anthologies: *Stand*, *Something Wicked* (EUP, Polygon), *Macallan Shorts* (Polygon), *Northwords*, *My Mum's A Punk* (anthology, Scottish Cultural Press), *Edinburgh Review*, *Mole*, *The Barcelona Review*, *The Herald*, *Deliberately Thirsty*, *Pretext* (Pen and Inc., University of East Anglia/New Writing Partnership), *Nova Scotia: Speculative Scottish Fiction* (Crescent), *Word Jig* (Hanging Loose Press, New York).

Several have been translated and some broadcast on BBC Radio 4, BBC Radio Scotland and the BBC World Service.

'The Sheriff and Susie and Swannie' was commissioned by the Scottish Arts Council for their website.

'Alice Kerr Went with Older Men' was commissioned by Sandstone Press for their website where an earlier version of this story appeared under the title 'Coming on Strong'.

The 'Five Fantastic Stories' were originally commissioned by the *Herald* newspaper where they first appeared.

An earlier version of 'Not Dead Yet, Lily?' was originally published in *Neonlit, Time Out Book of New Writing* (Quartet) under the title 'Alice'.

I would like to thank the Scottish Arts Council for a Writer's Bursary which allowed me time to complete this book.

Ron Butlin: an appreciation by Ian Rankin

I first met Ron Butlin in 1979. It was my first year at Edinburgh University, and I was a keen member of the undergraduate Poetry Society. We met weekly in an unprepossessing room at the Societies' Centre in Hill Place. At each session, a real-life poet (published and everything!) would read to us. But before they did, a selection of callow student poets would perform the role of warm-up acts. I'm not sure now if I played on the same bill as Ron, but I remember that at the end of the session many of us repaired to Potterrow Bar to drink beer and talk poetry. This was the real worth of the Poetry Society: a chance to spend time with professional writers. Ron was one of the first of these I'd ever met. At school, Carl MacDougall came in a few times to talk to my class, but that had been my only contact (fleeting at best). Now, poets like Ron became meat and drink to me.

Eventually, of course, I turned cannibal – lifting the title of one of Ron's stories ('The Tilting Room') for the name of a London pub in my novel *Watchman*, and having one of the characters in my novel *Black and Blue* quote from his first collection, *Creatures Tamed By Cruelty*. I bought a copy of that collection from Ron that night in Potterrow. It was published by Edinburgh University Student Publications Board, who would later (under the guise of Polygon Books) publish my own first novel. In his introduction to *Creatures Tamed by Cruelty*, Edwin Morgan says of Ron's poetry that it shows 'a considerable expertise and sophistication...one has the sense of an intelligence moving and probing and taking up positions behind subject matter that may be strongly emotional in itself'. I think the same can be said for all Ron's subsequent output, including the collection of stories you're about to read.

I think it's fair to say that in the late '70s and early '80s Ron was part of a trio of poets (the others being Andrew Greig and Brian McCabe) who to many of us were the Edinburgh scene. Irvine Welsh was still a gleam in his publisher's eye, and the only Edinburgh novelist seemed to be Muriel Spark, who hadn't lived in the city for over thirty years. What nourishment we fledglings got, we found in writers like Ron. However, after leaving university I lost touch with him, until the chance to review his first, devastating novel, *The Sound of My Voice*, gave me the opportunity to contact him again. I was in London by then, jobbing as a secretary at Middlesex Polytechnic, while he was travelling the world, seeking experiences which would translate themselves into poems and – increasingly – wonderful short stories. In my review of *The Sound of My Voice* I said that it was the kind of novel only a poet could write. This is true of Ron's stories, too. He constructs each one with infinite care, producing resonant images and layers of meaning, allowing the reader room to ruminate. As a result, there's something crystalline about his work. It is polished, and multi-faceted.

Take one of the stories in this present collection, for example: 'A Man Called Lockerbie'. The title hints at so much. We know the story must have something to do with the Lockerbie disaster, yet Ron chooses to focus elliptically on a railway worker with that surname. This character's connection with the tragedy remains tangential: he sells train tickets to mourners who are heading for the town. This gives a personal, human slant to something potentially overwhelming, and is a good example of Ron Butlin's approach to his stories. He finds the particular in the universal, and uses it to powerful effect.

He is also interested in history and mythology. One of his earliest published poems was a modern reworking of *Paradise Lost*. In this latest book, his story 'Temptations from an Ancient World' has fun reconstructing the likes of Orpheus and Jason and the Golden Fleece. This is because Ron Butlin is playful, too. He wears his learning lightly. This was made evident recently when his themed story collection *Vivaldi and the Number 3* was published. Ron's love of classical music came through, but that didn't stop him making merry with the re-imagined lives of famous composers, in some cases transplanting them to contemporary Scotland – an amusing enough trope in itself but enriched by the vein of compassion and humanity which is always present in Ron's work.

It always baffles me that the short story is such a neglected form – neglected by readers, I mean. Short stories, it seems to me, are perfect for our busy daily lives, adding nourishment to the bus queue or delayed train, a perfect accompaniment to a tea- or lunch break. The best of them cram a novel's worth of feeling into something much smaller but no less inspired and inspiring.

If you're reading Ron Butlin for the first time, you're about to discover a vigorous, challenging talent. If you already know his work, stand by for the latest treat.

How the angels fly in

Neither of his guests want to be here, that's obvious. Every time a cup or saucer clatters onto the hard shine of his formica table there's another awkward pause. But they're putting on a gallant show: compliments to his bachelor tidiness have been succeeded by Mark's hilarious account of his and the lovely Donna's rats-in-a-trap drive across town to get here this afternoon. Jordan catches the odd word, he is playing the host to perfection and appreciates their need for small talk. He is not a cruel man.

It's been twenty-five years since he was at school with Mark, or rather with the boy Mark once was; he'd never met the lovely Donna before. They'd been going into Woolworth's when he caught sight of them: a quick 'Long-time-no-see', an invitation for them to drop round, and a follow-up phone call he'd made a few days later – and they hadn't a chance. Too polite for their own good. But having agreed to come, however reluctantly, they will make the most of this opportunity to view him – let's be clear about their motives even if they themselves aren't.

Between sips of tea, Mark continues gabbling on about the new one-way system through town, the new parking problems. Sometimes Jordan turns the sound down, as it were, and just watches: with no words to distract him, his guests' nervous mannerisms and gestures are a giveaway. Mark, for example, keeps turning ever so slightly towards the door that leads to the hall and upstairs – not too difficult to work out what's going on in his mind. As for the lovely Donna, with her thick black hair and nice breasts already saying more than enough, she needn't speak if she doesn't want to. She looks uncomfortable though, and avoids meeting his eye.

'Another piece of shortbread, Donna?' He smiles and pushes the plate in her direction. Being a well brought up little Miss she will accept the kindliness of his manner and might even be feeling sorry for him. At school Mark had the right haircut, the right jeans, the right trainers; he went around with other *right* boys like himself, the ones who played football and had girlfriends. Jordan rarely addressed any of 'the boys' in case they snubbed him; he hated them, and would have given anything to be one of them. Since returning to the town a year ago he has run into a fair number of those 'boys', usually on a Saturday, in their casual weekend sweatshirts and with wife and kids in tow. A few moments' chat and they can't wait to get away. No one was ever going to call round to say hello, that's for sure.

By now, Mark's monologue has turned quite frantic, a gabble to ward off the silence that has long become part of the house itself. In normal circumstances the rigours of traffic systems, off-zone parking and the like provide the familiar shallows where the grown-up 'boys' of this world paddle around for all they're worth, splashing loudly to make a reassuring noise for themselves. But the circumstances that have brought them here today are not normal, and so: gabble, gabble, gabble while looking far across the green formica to the deeper waters where he, Jordan, calmly gazes back at them in his unrivalled experience of life and, more importantly, of death.

'More tea?' He makes sure he's already started pouring before the lovely Donna has a chance to refuse. 'Well, Donna, and how do you like living in our town? How long have you been here now?'

She likes it. It's a nice town. She's been here fourteen years.

'So long? Almost a native, eh! The new Riverview Estate I think you said. Beautiful houses in a beautiful setting – the old army barracks stood there when Mark and I were at school. Waste of a prime building site, it was. You'll be well settled in now, I expect?'

Yes, the neighbours are friendly but not too much, if he knows what she means. He nods. Near enough the town centre but still quiet and by itself. Another interested nod.

And so on. And so on. And so on...

When Jordan feels ready he will start them on the next stage of their visit, a tour of the house, both floors, and ending up in the room directly above the kitchen where they are now seated, enjoying tea and shortbread. Meanwhile he'll sit listening to their aimless chit-chat and his own equally aimless responses. Best of all would be to raise his hand for silence, and to hold everything just there: the conversation stopped in mid-sentence. A snap of the fingers and, transported as if by magic, the three of them would be upstairs, staring into that part of hell he had the courage to enter twenty-five years ago, and has been trapped in ever since.

Instead, he has to let the chit-chat go on while the hall clock chimes another quarter of an hour done away with. He sits and they sit.

Tea and shortbread finished, it is time to turn the gabble off at source with a friendly, 'Would you like to see round?'

Then, before they can make some excuse about leaving or putting him to unnecessary trouble, he stands up and motions Mark and the lovely Donna to rise from their places at the formica.

'The house was built at the end of the nineteenth century; my parents added the extension.'

And with this casual mentioning of his parents – intended as a token of reassurance – the tour has begun.

He ushers them into the dining-room to inspect the marble

fireplace, the splendid shutters, the bow-windows and finally – star attraction! – the vast mahogany sideboard. What craftsmanship! He points out the delicacy with which every rose-petal and spray has been painstakingly carved, the intricate harmony of the different grains, the integrity of the entire piece as having been constructed without nail or glue. Naturally he makes no comment on the cabinets smelling of mould, nor does he draw attention to the empty drawers whose velvet casings must have been stripped of the family cutlery not long after the evening he entered his parents' bedroom.

There are none of the customary framed photographs, if that's why the lovely Donna is glancing around the room. Weddings, christenings, anniversaries – his family has nothing to prove anymore. Or hasn't that been explained to her yet? Poor Donna, wherever she looks she will be disappointed: polished surfaces reflect back a china shepherdess, a candlestick in its brass holder, dustbowls of pottery. The small talk's been hastily resumed in response to the hollow echoing of their footsteps on the room's uncarpeted floor. Feeling mischievous he interrupts with a question:

'And do you have any children?'

At once the lovely Donna stiffens, then almost immediately relaxes again. So, she *does* know. Mark must have told her after their unexpected meeting last week. Or did the coward wait until the very last minute, until they were driving up and down the one-way streets to get here? *By the way, darling, there's something about Jordan I think I should tell you…*

The abruptness of his question, with its darker implications, was perfectly timed and has caught them both completely unawares. There is a somewhat uncertain 'Not yet' from Mark which is tempered by detail upon detail of a lifeplan calculated, so it seems, to take him and the lovely Donna safely into late middle-age and beyond. A lifeplan – these paddlers in the shallows! They're out

– 4 –

of their depth now all right! Glancing at each other in a way he's not supposed to know anything about, the pair of them! For they are *a couple*, they are special and have drawn a circle – completely invisible to the likes of him, of course – around themselves to keep themselves beyond harm. Do they really believe that team-spirit, haircuts, designer labels, parking restrictions, marriage and the rest of it are enough to guide them and keep them safe? Such good, good people. Having brought them here he will show them what really lies inside their careful little circle.

He was thirteen when he made his way along the upstairs corridor, eyes half-closed to conceal from himself the sharpness of the carving knife he held in his hand. There was no sound from his parents' bedroom: the madness that filled the house day after day with its screams, its rage and despair must have been pausing for breath. He reached for the door handle. Until then he had tried his best to fit in: to read the signs and anticipate convincing demonstrations of fear, of repentance, or whatever was required; always ready to give a whispered 'Yes' in answer to every crazy accusation while silencing within himself the 'No' screaming to be heard. Had their madness at last become his own? Was that what had made him slide open the sideboard drawer, lift out the carving knife from its velvet setting and come upstairs? He'd been nothing more than a child when, with tears running down his face, he hacked his way to the heart of the only circle he had known.

And so, twenty-five years later: left hand on the banisters, best foot forward, and up he goes leading the way. Faded yellow wallpaper, re-patterned by colourful streaks of damp, to his right; and to his left the solidity of varnished oak. He urges his guests forward, his voice talking about underfelt, carpets, redecorating, rewiring… and their voices dutifully fill in the gaps he leaves for them.

'I'm thinking of having the doors stripped back to the natural wood.'

'We did that ourselves a couple of years ago. Lots of work but worth it, wasn't it, Donna?'

'Yes. Looks nice when it's finished.'

And so the landing is reached.

Then the room opposite. His voice jostling theirs into response to make sure every single second is accounted for. Their unspoken question: *Was it here?*

Along the corridor.

The next room is reached.

Then further along the corridor.

The last room.

His voice continues firm, steady, obliging; he explains that he is preparing things for the decorators. He points out the unpainted walls, the blocked-up fireplace and the emptiness where his parents' furniture had stood: the chairs, dressing table, wardrobe, their bed. That much he tells them in a voice that doesn't falter.

He pauses, and can hardly believe it when what he has most hoped for at this point actually occurs: a sudden and visible arrest of feeling on the faces of these, his very first guests. They are deeply moved. For several seconds no one speaks. He waits. They know what happened here. Surely they can sense what showing them this room must mean to him?

The lovely Donna has taken a few hesitant steps forward. She's pointing to the skylight set into the sloping roof, it's rusted solid and stuck slightly open. She's said something.

'Pardon?'

'That's how the angels fly in,' she repeats. 'When I was little that's what my granddad used to say when someone had left a window open.' She's looking at him, and actually smiling.

'Angels?' What's the woman talking about? What's she doing here if that's all she has to say? 'Angels?'

He should calm himself or in a minute he'll be stammering.

'Yes, they were invisible, of course, but granddad said if we listened hard enough we would hear their wings as they flew around us.'

He can feel sweat standing out on his brow, clamminess on his hands. He's started trembling.

Mark grins: 'That would be something, eh, Donna!'

Can't they see what's happening to him? He tenses himself but the shaking's taken over his whole body. Can't they see it? Can't they do something?

No. They're gabbling and grinning and giving advice on redecoration.

A slight draught comes into the room, bringing with it the scent of cherry blossom from the back garden – a sickly, choking stench. If the skylight wasn't set so high he'd make the pair of them watch him jam it shut. Then he'd frogmarch them out of the room, along the corridor, down the stairs and away to wherever they'd come from.

He needs stepladders, tools. He'll wrench the window back into place, nail it shut, board it up if he has to. No more angels, no more guests.

He holds the door open for them to leave. He must hurry. Quickly, before the cherry blossom gets stronger and fills the whole house so he cannot breathe. Quickly, before the angels come, the lightest touch of whose wings brings the threat of forgiveness.

Colours

At first, every day was the same and afterwards I'd fall into bed exhausted. An hour later I'd be jackknifed out of sleep, ready to scream the house down.

Screaming's a therapeutic 'plus', no doubt, but not a real option at three in the morning. So I lay and held my breath, it felt like, while the strokes of the church bell forced me another quarter of an hour closer to getting up, getting dressed and starting the day after you were killed all over again. Every chime and echo gave the darkness a few seconds' weight – like a paving stone, let's say, where I could stop and rest before taking the next slow-motion step towards daylight. At 3 a.m. there'd be fifteen paving stones still to go – I'd be wide awake and dead beat on every single one of them.

Washing/cleaning/cooking/laundry/teaching/shopping/preparing lessons/marking exercises/the boys' tears/the boys' tantrums/ chaos. It was when I was going out of my mind one long night towards the end of that first month that I came up with a plan to stop the chaos.

The following day was a Sunday. Once we'd returned from visiting your grave in the afternoon, I stood each boy up against the wall to be measured: William, 1 metre 17 cm; Michael, 1.27m; Frank, 1.32m. That done, and with the through-doors wide open,

I marched each of them in turn the length of the house (35.74 metres there and back), and timed them. I insisted they maintained a straight line and a steady pace throughout. At first they thought it a great laugh and chased each other up and down the hall as if it was some kind of race. I soon put them right. Once they understood how painstakingly I'd done the calculations, they respected my seriousness of purpose. William, as fair-haired and sweet-tempered as yourself, proved the most biddable and kept to his prescribed rate of 3.25 mph with metronomic regularity. Because of his tendency to be easily distracted, Michael needed shouted at. Frank, threatening adolescence in a couple of years, managed his set rate (3.75 mph) only when I paced alongside him, blowing my whistle every few steps.

That first night together twelve years ago, I never slept either; nor did you. We kissed, undressed, made love, talked, made love again then, all at once, it was time for the breakfast tea and toast. A whole night gone with nothing to show for it but your steamed-up windows – and the two of us in love! Until then I'd thought love was a woman's country where men wandered in and out on limited-stay visas, sightseeing and collecting souvenirs, but never quite managing to settle. That one night changed everything. A kind of soft-focus madness began: I turned up at your flat the following evening with yellow roses, 'to match your hair'. Having trimmed them to fit, you put them in a vase: 'I can look at them and think of you when you're not here.' Not there? My idea was that from then on I lived in your heart...

The days that followed were dream-days when I sat blissful in a roomful of eight-year-old dinosaurs and pterodactyls without even trying to nail them to their seats. Benign from the heart outwards, I left them free to roam among the desks, like so many anarchic miracles come back from before the Ice Age screeching and swooping with life. A man in love, set down in the mayhem of prehistory. Oblivious to the ravages of fifty million years' evolution happening around me, I'd appear to be cutting out paper dinosaurs and pasting them down in the Dinosaur Checklist when really I'd be imagining your arms around me, tasting your skin, feeling your tongue against mine.

I'm still a man in love, so why can't I feel like that now? Why is there nothing or, even less than nothing – only your absence?

Now that we have no car we've regressed back to public transport. Unfortunately, the boys' bus goes one way and mine the opposite. Hence every morning's frantic rush. Hence my plan. Measurements and calculations completed, it swung into action on Monday morning and worked a treat: the previous night's dishes still in the sink, the previous three days' unwashed laundry still on the floor, I was running late when I got the boys lined up at the door – three paratroopers ready for the big drop – and set them off at the necessary intervals. By going separately they didn't interfere with each other's progress and so kept more or less to time. That was the plan. Three perfect days followed. Then came the fourth. The bins put out, the shopping list discovered, I was running even later when I locked up the house and marched myself to my bus-stop. When my bus went past their stop I glanced out the window as usual. The boys were still there. At once, I jumped to my feet, rang the emergency bell, explained to the driver and was off the bus within seconds. I returned to where the three of them stood in a neat line, satchels on their backs, grins on their faces. William clutching his gym kit in a Tesco bag. He smirked up at me:

'It was early.'

The other two held their sides and howled with laughter. But not for long.

The next bus wasn't for another hour. I'd have to phone their school, then phone my own. Teaching cover would have to be arranged, timetables altered. I walked them home ready to start all over again.

That evening I wrote to the bus company. My first letter of complaint ever. I told them I'd done everything possible on my side: I'd timed the boys, timetabled their separate mornings up to the moment each of them arrived at the stop – only to find the Eastern City Bus Company hadn't done its part, the driver in particular. I pitched it strong, presenting my case and the attendant circumstances with reasonable fairness. Afterwards I made a special trip to the post box at the street corner.

Every so often since then, it seems someone hits the PAUSE button and the momentum I've managed to build up is abruptly stopped. I have to grab the edge of the table or the back of a chair to steady myself. Then the button's released and everything returns to normal. If the boys notice anything they never say.

I wrote again the following week, then the week after.

Exactly two months to the day after you were killed I decided it was high time the boys and I wrote a joint letter to the bus company as my previous ones had gone unanswered. During lunch I explained how important this was and how we had to demonstrate to the owners that their duty lay in ensuring their drivers' strict adherence to what, after all, was their own timetable. There could be no excuses. Each of us would tell his own story in his own words, explaining how the bus's leaving too soon that morning had affected his life. William, for example, had missed gym and that was the day they were picking the under-nines football team; I had arranged to take a class to the museum, and so forth...Having cleared away the dishes we would sit at the dining table, each with a piece of paper and a pen. Stick to the facts I told them, but stress the personal. William, as the youngest, was to be allowed a set of coloured crayons should he wish to illustrate his letter.

Before going in the room to join them I paused a moment outside. A pleasing, busy sound was coming to me through the door: the scraping of someone's chair, whispers as the boys discussed what they were planning to write. It was a good moment.

I pushed open the door and went in. Three faces were staring up at me. Trusting, hopeful faces. Another good moment.

I gave out the pens and paper and was about to go over some final instructions before giving them an opportunity to ask any last questions when, from over at the window, I became aware of an agitation on the outside of the glass. A small bird was beating its wings trying to get in. I crossed the room and pulled the curtains shut. There had to be no distraction from the task at hand. I felt my way back through the darkness to the doorway, clicked on the light and gave a slight cough to indicate we were ready to begin.

'Okay, boys: Top right hand corner: our address and today's date – 19-2-06.'

Frank finished this first, then Michael. The three of us waited in silence for William to blot his way to the last digit and put his tongue back in his mouth. Then we continued.

'Left hand side, on the line below the date line. Write: *Dear Sir*, capital *D*, capital *S*.'

The clattering and drumming of the wings seemed more frantic than ever, but I was glad to note the boys paid no attention. Their three faces – Frank's first, then Michael's and, nearly a whole minute later, William's, eventually looked up from the paper.

'A good start means the job will go well.' I smiled at them. 'Now, when you're ready, in your own time and your own words, continue your letter.'

Three heads bent down once more and three pens were poised to begin. Before a word was written, however, the boys immediately moved into exam-mode, shielding their work from each other so there could be no chance of copying. It was a pleasure to witness such commitment, such enthusiasm. I'd wait until things were well and truly started, then begin my own letter. The bird must have flown away. Within seconds a calmness had settled over the room; and I was almost smiling when I took up my pen.

We might have gone swimming that day, or played football, or gone for a bicycle ride, or stayed at home. Or anything. Instead –

I'd been accelerating past the Fairmilehead sliproad when I began waxing teacherly about the mystery trip I'd thought up that morning. No one else knew where we were going. The whole thing was my idea.

Mine alone.

The boys were in the back seat performing low-volume animal impersonations to pass the time, you were sitting next to me and had just asked me to give a few clues about our destination.

'Well, Joan, it's not far out of Edinburgh. It's called a farm, but isn't really. There's only the one kind of thing there – but there'll be hundreds and thousands of them, and more colours than you can imagine.' To tease you, I added: 'Some of them migrate here from Spain, from Mexico even.'

You were looking so puzzled I couldn't resist one final clue: 'They fly all the way, but you'd never believe it.'

Out of the corner of my eye I could see you were half-laughing. You must have been humouring me all along because a moment later you smiled:

Your voice came from beside me, from the point of impact:

'Butterflies?'

Fragments of glass were rising in a broken-coloured shower that for a split-second seemed to hang motionless in front of me.

From behind came the boys' screaming.

This letter was going to be the best yet. Polite, but a real stinger. I leant forward to begin.

Then stopped. My sheet was already half-covered with writing.

How had that happened? I glanced up to see the curtains standing open once more. William was now the only other person at the table, the only other person still in the room even. What the hell was going on? He was looking at me, his face a smear of blue ink and tears.

'They're outside, you told them to go outside,' he blubbered.

I'd told them?

'Have they finished their letters?' Without meaning to I shouted at him.

He rushed from the room. I heard the back door slam.

I began reading what was in front of me. A mess. A furious scrawl of obscenities. Was that handwriting really mine? Here and there the writing was scored through and the paper ripped.

With what seemed a great effort I managed to pull myself to my feet. None of the boys had managed to get anywhere near finished. A few lines, nothing more. Well, they could finish them later. I smoothed out the sheets and started stacking them, mine at the bottom, then Frank's, then Michael's; William's I placed on top. He'd not written a single word – it was a drawing of three small stick-boys and their stick-man of a father chasing after a bus as it disappeared towards the edge of the paper. I was about to scrunch it into a ball when a detail caught my eye: he'd made the driver a woman. A woman with long yellow hair.

It's nearly midnight. I've returned to the dining-room to pull the curtains as I always do, last thing; and I've just noticed a hairline of refracted light running across one of the panes. The left-hand window's cracked. Surely that bird beating its wings couldn't have broken the glass? I would have heard it at the time, wouldn't I?

But there it is. I stare at the tracery of fractured colours.

I want to shut the curtains.

I want to turn and leave the room.

I want to close the door behind me. To lock it.

Instead, I remain standing here in front of the window, quite unable to move, half-expecting the impossible – that these lacerated reds, vermillions and dusk-blues might gradually, and with the very slightest quiver of unsettledness, begin to lift themselves free from the glass...

'Butterflies?' you asked.

And I am able to answer you at last.

Not dead yet, Lily?

With the approach of the thunderstorm Lily was growing more and more restless. As the air became clammier and heavier, every breath stuck in her lungs like sweat. Outside, the sky had darkened to blue-black. The window was open but no draught came in. Four in the afternoon, midsummer almost, and dark enough indoors to have to switch on the light. But she wouldn't.

Instead, having struggled to her feet, she stood in the airless front room listening to herself gasp for breath – she'd better wait a moment before setting off to the kitchen for a drink of water. She didn't want to have the likes of Mrs MacDonald come in to find her keeled over at last. Sometimes it felt as if the whole street was waiting for her to go. All these neighbourly visits about nothing in particular, except to check she'd not died in her sleep. They were being kind, and she supposed she was grateful, but there was always the unspoken pause, the split-second's refocusing of a glance that betrayed the real question:

Not dead yet?

Well, she appreciated their concern, but fuck them.

Yes, that was the only language to use. In the last few weeks Lily had discovered the relish of bad language. One morning she'd been woken by Mrs Miller phoning to ask, after the 'not-dead-yet?' pause, if she wanted something from the shop. She'd said no, then hung up.

Now for breakfast, she'd thought, breakfast, bloody breakfast. As she pulled on her dressing-gown she'd started muttering to herself:

'Bloody breakfast, bloody, bloody, bloody, bloody breakfast.'

It felt good, stimulating. Like a vigorous marching tune in her head. There she stood in front of the mirror: a kindly-looking, white-haired, elderly woman, frail but dignified – those were no doubt the sorts of words her neighbours used when talking about her – and all the time behind the benevolent smile she was hammering out full-force, 'BLOODY, BLOODY, BLOODY, BLOODY breakfast.' Then she'd grinned to herself – and she'd not done that in months.

In a short time the *bloody*s had given way to *hell*s, and the *hell*s to *damn*s – but getting into *fuck*s had been her big breakthrough. It was after the postman went by a couple of days ago: *No letters, well fuck him!* she'd thought, then announced,

'Fuck him! Fuck him! Fuck him!' to the clock, the empty armchair and a whole clutch of wedding photographs. Stopping herself in time from getting too loud. Not because it might shock the MacDonalds and Millers or whoever might be passing. She didn't care about them; it was simply because she didn't really want to share these words with anyone: coming from her they were hers, and hers alone.

But her words weren't working today. 'Fucking storm, fucking storm,' she kept repeating as she stood in the kitchen letting the tap run for coolness, but didn't feel any better. The water tasted heavy and tepid. She'd go into the garden.

The sky was much blacker than before with everything beneath gripped in sharp, shadowless light, and the air so sluggish she almost had to push her way through it. Nothing seemed to move out here. Across the street she could see the MacDonalds, a group of stuffed figures crouched in a family circle around their patio-table. Who were the MacDonalds, who were the Millers? Where had they come from? Where had any of the people in the street come from with their tracksuits, their baggy shorts, their baseball caps, their mobile phones and their internets?

The heaviness in the air seemed to have turned that bush by her front gate completely rigid. When she gave one of the branches a tug, it shook – she could tell – unwillingly. Her neighbour's brand-new spade was propped just within reach; without thinking what she was doing, she picked it up. Its metal edge clanged against the stone path, a *clang* that seemed to fill the street. Too bad. She clanged it once more and her reward was five MacDonald faces panned in her direction.

As she leant towards the bush its perfume stuck to her skin and, in its sultriness, the scent seemed almost a solid thing. Perhaps, the air being so still, if she removed the plant and its scent, she could fit herself into the gap left behind, and so withdraw from a world filled with strangers bringing their strange ways.

She started spading out earth. Not so hard really, but with every thrust and lift she had to stop to catch her breath. There was sweat trickling down her face and back. She paused for a moment to wipe her eyes clear – and *there*, up on their hind legs, were a couple of MacDonalds staring over at her. The bigger of them, a wobble of pink flesh, baldness and glasses, was already starting in her direction.

She carried on digging. Not that she could remember what the plant was called, nor what anything much was called these days, only that some things were alive and some things weren't. Really, who cared? One good tug and she'd have it free.

The wobbly MacDonald was standing at her gate: 'Mrs Williams! Hello there, Mrs Williams!'

Should she pretend to have gone deaf?

Yes.

Taking a good grip of the stem with both hands, feet braced for the effort, she closed her eyes for the Big Tug.

'Hello there, Mrs Williams! That's a lovely lilac you've got there: can I help you at all?'

The bush came out more easily than she'd expected, almost first pull, making her stagger a couple of steps backwards. She threw it to one side then picked up the spade again.

'You really should be resting in weather like this, Mrs Williams. What are you doing?'

Before she could stop herself she'd replied, 'Digging my fucking grave. At my age what the fuck else would I be doing?'

When she next looked up the MacDonald had gone.

Indoors, it was almost dark. She went through to the kitchen to wash her hands, then sat down as the first rumble of thunder sounded. Heavy drops of rain began spattering the window. Feeling a bit tired after all that digging, she might just have a short nap now – while she was in the mood.

Kindness

(remembering Dorothy)

Men became dogs, Lily had decided. From day one of Frank's retirement, he'd been perpetually *in attendance*: the domestic pet always wanting to be talked to, listened to, patted, played with... and quite unable to do anything on his own. She loved him more than ever even, as she saw how vulnerable, how helpless almost, he became. Especially at the end.

Probably because today is the only day of the week that matters anymore, and she's about to go out, Lily finds herself expecting him to be waiting for her at the front door — in his hat, coat and polished shoes — hoping to be taken for a walk. She's just finished giving her hair a last-minute brush. Of course Frank *can't* be there — and it would be weakness, plain and simple, to glance down the corridor to check.

For several seconds she stands quite motionless in front of the mirror, wanting to whisper his name. Then stops herself. But why not? There's no one watching. Why shouldn't she let her lips move as they clearly long to, and say *Frank* out loud? Why on earth shouldn't she? There's no one in the house but her, as she knows only too well.

If Lily can be said to have a hobby, it's Special Offer Day at the local supermarket. As she turns the corner of the street, she begins speeding up. In addition to 'Give-Aways for the Greenhouse', this week's Special Offer leaflet has promised 'a Christmas Tree to Last a Lifetime' and an 'Energy-Saving Miracle': a portable shower-unit that allows the used water to be re-circulated thanks to a hand-pump attachment. Sonya, her eco-bore of a daughter, will be getting it for her birthday, and liking it.

'Mrs Williams?'

A car has drawn up beside her.

'Going into town, Mrs Williams?'

It's Helen Miller. Her husband Tom – six foot of awkward silence broken only by a growl of moustache – is driving. A kindly man, though. They are a kindly couple.

'Only to the supermarket.'

'Like a lift? It's a warm day.'

'It's not far. I can manage, thank you.'

'Of course you can, Mrs Williams. We just thought…'

Being sure to take in both Millers and the family moustache in one overall smile, she leans towards the car: 'It's very kind of you, but if I'm still moving, I know I'm still alive!'

A few more smiles are batted back and forth before Lily can continue on her way.

She spends nearly an hour in the supermarket. Special Offers take time…Finally she settles on the extendable Christmas tree with a pointed metal tip (safety cap attached) for the bubble-wrapped angel (enclosed), and the portable shower-unit. She also buys some meat and vegetables.

At the checkout she asks if she can leave her purchases and pick them up on her way back from the baker's. No problem.

She's hardly gone twenty yards when she hears someone calling after her: 'Old lady! Old lady!'

Naturally she keeps going.

A teenage boy in supermarket uniform comes running to catch up with her. He's holding out her bags: the foodstuffs in one, the shower head sticking out of the other and the Christmas tree under his arm like a rolled-up umbrella.

'Your things. I thought maybe you'd forgotten – I mean, maybe you had...' He stops, in confusion.

'The girl said she'd keep them for me.' She manages to give a reassuring smile: 'but that was very kind of you. Thank you.'

The boy nods. Then blushes.

'I'll pick them up shortly,' she explains. 'On my way back from the baker's.' Smile number two's an effort. Much tireder suddenly, she carries on into town.

A warm day and getting warmer. By the time she reaches the next block, she feels that every step's a step further from home. She needs to rest for a few moments, she needs some shade. Eventually she reaches the awning outside Aladdin's Cave, that treasure-trove of household novelties: full of Special Offers, and tempting as sin. Though what does sin matter to her anymore? If there was a God, she'd decided at Frank's funeral, then He had a hell of a lot to answer for. Mysterious ways, right enough. As she'd stood at the open graveside, almost two years ago to the very day and as hot, she'd found herself counting up all those wasted Sunday mornings, and all that wasted collection money. And for what? Helplessly she'd watched Frank's last desperate efforts to crawl up a slope that just got steeper and steeper; his screaming and weeping with pain; the drugs, the plastic tubes and oxygen; bits of him packing up, bits of him rotting while she could do nothing but sit by his bedside, and look on.

As they'd walked back to the cemetery gates the minister had turned to her: 'Your husband will be at peace now, in a better place.'

Her sudden fury: 'I want Frank *here*, with me!'

The touch of the minister's hand on her shoulder: 'God is Love and Mercy. Let us remember that Our Lord Jesus Christ, His only begotten Son, was sacrificed so that we—'

'A few hours on the cross was nothing to what my man had to suffer this last year.' Shaking herself free: 'His whole life, and *that's* what it came to. If God planned it, he should have thought of gas chambers – would have been kinder.'

The minister's face and neck were already red-raw, she was pleased to notice, and showing the promise of a nasty sunburn: 'Mrs Williams! You don't know what you're saying. You're angry, you're distressed. I understand. God understands and –

That was when she'd walked off.

The following Sunday she'd gone to a car-boot sale instead. Her first. For the fiver she'd have put into the collection she came home with a cuckoo-clock that turned out to announce the hours quite at random. Sometimes the cuckoo remained silent for a whole day, then made up for it with a burst of mechanical shooting out, then in, then out again while screeching at full pitch till his spring ran down. She nailed his little wooden house up in the hall. Wind him up, she'd thought, and the poor demented thing at least did his best – which was more than she could say for God.

It's pleasantly cool under the shop awning. She's in no hurry and can allow herself a comforting glance at the novelties displayed in the window of Aladdin's Cave: the elephant-shaped teapot that pours out through its trunk, the Eiffel Tower toast rack, the mosque-shaped alarm clock...

'Mrs Williams, how pleased to see you.'

'Good day, Mustapha.'

'Long time no look round. Welcome, please.'

'No, thank you. Just window-shopping today.'

'You're tired. One minute, please. I bring chair.' Before she can stop him he's disappeared into the shop.

What's she to do? She doesn't want to sit down, to be fussed over, to be stared at by every passer-by, but she can't just walk away…Or can she?…But what about the next time she passes his shop? Or will she always have to go the long way round?

'Sit please.'

Mustapha has unfolded a garden seat for her. She sits down.

'Thank you, you're very kind.' She's having to force out the words.

'A glass of water?'

She's not a *memsahib*, is she? Mustapha is simply being friendly, she reminds herself, *she's* the one seeing him as a deferential clasp of hands, a bow and a turban. What's the matter with her today?

'No thank you, Mustapha. I'll be fine in a minute. Busy, are you?'

'Busy, yes. But troubled also. Every morning I say let there not be trouble – no Paki-calling, no broken windows,' he looks down at the pavement between them. 'And worse things.'

Her hand resting on the chair-arm, the thickness of the padded cushions – she feels so very, very comfortable. The difficulty's going to be getting herself up and beginning the walk to the baker's before the long trek home.

'I'm sorry to hear that.' She shakes her head. 'Even around here…?'

'Here, everywhere. Not skinheads anymore. Nice people can be not so very nice.'

Beyond the edge of shade the street is all glare, a harshness of light cut into strips of hot pavement and hot road; when cars come round the corner, their windscreens catch the sun with a stab of sudden brightness. The very thought of walking out again into that heat…

She must have nodded off. Only for a few seconds, surely. Mustapha is looking at her, clearly waiting for her to say something.

'You've been very kind, Mustapha. Thank you.' She gets to her feet. ' I really must be getting back. My daughter's expecting me.' The lie comes easily. 'Goodbye, Mustapha.' She steps into the heat and drags herself away.

'Don't forget your change, dear.'

The casualness of the assistant's tone hits her like a blow across the face, the kind of blow to make her eyes water. Or is she about to burst into tears? Not tears, she wills herself, not in public. She takes the money and blunders out of the shop, letting the door slam behind her.

What a state she's got herself into…Better to calm down, take a deep breath, eyes forward, left foot, right foot…Avoiding Mustapha's shop, she'll go back to the supermarket, collect her shopping, then carry on straight home.

Only a dozen or so yards down the road, and she's halted. The bread. With all that mix-up over the money she's gone and left the wrapped loaf on the counter.

She hesitates, but can't go back. Why doesn't one of the customers come out after her? She's ready to smile and be grateful – and this time she'll really mean it.

'Can I help you…?'

A girl of about ten is standing beside her: blonde hair, untroubled blue eyes gazing up into her face. Not the least bit shy. 'Can I help you across the road?'

'No, thank you. I was just—'

Already the eyes have veered away to one side: 'If you're fine, then…' The girl's walking off.

A split-second later, Lily calls after her: 'Just a minute!' For here's the solution to her problem: a girl so blonde, so blue-eyed and brimming with kindness will surely be only too happy to go back to the baker's for her.

'Just a minute, little girl! Please!'

A bus goes roaring past drowning out her words. The girl's continued up the street. Too late.

The energy-saving shower in one bag, the meat, vegetables and supermarket bread in the other, and the extendible Christmas tree tucked under her arm, Lily trudges up to the pedestrian crossing. By edging sideways she's managed to press the button with her elbow. The sign beneath lights up:

WAIT.

Well, she's waiting. In less than five minutes she'll be home. Which is just as well: if she has to manage one more smile, has to come out with one more *thank you, I'm so grateful / thank you, you're so kind*, she'll be screaming at people. Between that, and her tiredness, and the heat…She can imagine the coolness she'll soon be stepping into at home. She'll lock the front door behind her, change into her indoor clothes, make a pot of tea, switch on the radio. And relax.

No other pedestrian in sight. No traffic either.

She's about to cross when she feels one of the plastic bag handles beginning to stretch. That's the last thing she needs. She takes a firmer grip.

Pip-pip-pip: the lights have changed to the green man. A car, a sporty-looking piece of red flashiness thud-thudding with music, has been forced to brake hard and stop. Out of the corner of her eye she sees the driver – shaved head, or maybe bald, and oval like a peanut. He's glaring at her. Let him.

You've got a lot more time ahead of you than I have, she wants to yell at him.

Instead, as she steps off the pavement, a wave of total exhaustion sweeps over her. The other side of the road seems impossibly far. The heat from the car bonnet's like an oven door standing open. Her left foot, then her right…

With Frank beside her, walking to the shops together, walking home together, spending the day together, and the day after…

With Frank, without Frank…Her left foot, then her right…

'Hey there, missus!'

The *thud-thud's* been abruptly turned down and the driver's shouting at her. She feels so tired that if she stops to turn and look, she'll collapse into a heap on the road. So, so tired: her left foot forward, and then her right…

Like a lash cutting across her back: 'Come on, grandma, the lights have changed. Move it!'

Her left foot forward, and then her right…

Again the lash: 'Move it, I said!' And yet again: 'Your old man'll've dropped dead waiting for his dinner!'

Suddenly the lash feels like a charge of electricity, a bolt of pure energy that surges through her. She wheels round to face him: 'You – you – *peanut-head*!' She puts down her bags.

A double-decker's passing only a few feet away. She ignores it.

Peanut-head revs his engine: 'Come on, missus. The lights. Out the road!'

Having removed the safety cap, she extends this week's Special Offer to its full length and holds it out in front of her like a lance. The metal tip flashes in the sun.

She takes aim. 'Merry Christmas!'

Then rams it in full-force.

Peanut-head's leaning out of his window.

'What–? What the fuck're you doing, you old cow?'

A final twist for luck. There's a rush of escaping air. A most pleasing *hiss*.

A moment later, Lily has stepped lightly onto the opposite pavement. She pauses for a moment to enjoy a last, satisfying look: the long line of stalled traffic is getting longer by the second. Some drivers are hooting their horns, some are shouting and waving their fists. Peanut-head's standing beside his car, staring down at his flat tyre.

She takes a good grip of her bags, turns and strides briskly off.

At her front door she gets out her key. She knows she was in the wrong. Such ingratitude, after all the kindness the world has shown her. She shakes her head, beginning to feel sorry for what she did. Only a little sorry, though.

The key turns and her front door opens. She's home.

itsmichael

Being friendly to Sailor and the rest of them for the next six hours will be like having a knife turned in me.

The bar door opens. Outside in the yard I can see starlings and sparrows scattered along the power lines like so many crochets on a stave. Not that I'll get a chance to hear a single note any of them'll make...

The door's slammed shut again – no yard, no sparrows, no starlings – and I'm left with Sailor, that rust-can on two legs, wanting served.

I pour his pint, ring up the till and pass him his change, all the while hearing the two of us discuss Scotland's game tonight against Morocco. I watch his red beard leech itself to the rim of his glass for several seconds – and half the pint's gone. His drunken eyes pick me out from the rest of the bar fittings:

'The Mock Turtles, Michael? No problem. Draw'll see us through.'

My voice answers him.

The phone starts to ring.

Wee Cammie's hammering the lino floor with his pool cue; Dinger's clapping his hands, his cue tucked underarm, giving him the elegance and poise, briefly, of Fred Astaire. Recently, every moment in this place has become a still from a black-

and-white film – not like the real colours gliding and fanning themselves to full stretch in their open-air cage. Another three hours till I can take a short break and go out into the evening coolness, cross the yard to the wire netting, unlock the door and step in. They'll flutter around me, and the smallest will settle on my outstretched hands.

The phone keeps ringing. I should pick it up. I hear the phone ringing and ringing while my voice offers Sailor an explanation of the FIFA points system.

Because, of course, what I really want to do is take hold of the phone and pull so hard it comes away from the wall, and the whole wall comes away, and the bar and the conversation I'm having with Sailor and each one of the last few terrible days I've lived through – pull and pull until the entire black-and-white film's peeled back, leaving me here alone but for the dartings of red, green, yellow, and electric blue.

Instead: Sailor's red beard gives us both a rest by coming down sudden as a tropical sunset on a lagoon of McEwan's. I turn away. The phone stops in mid-ring.

I'd been on my way to the Craigbar Cash & Carry for the week's cigarettes, crisps and so on. At the top of the hill before turning into the main road to town I remembered about the Cash & Carry card. Had I taken it out of the till? I was sure I had, but couldn't recall actually doing so. I must have, and yet…

Just before the Dunmore bridge I pulled into the lay-by, checked my wallet, my pockets. No card. They all know me at the C&C but that, of course, would mean nothing to their computer. So, like it or not, I had to turn the car and head back.

It's a modest hotel we have, three bedrooms, a small dining-room and the one bar. With no guests midweek the place was deserted when I returned: everything neat and clean, the bar mats centred, the counters wiped and spotless, bar taps with cloths spread over them, the one time of the day the air's breathable. I rang up NO SALE and reached into the back of the till drawer. No card.

Was it because I thought I'd lost it or because time was getting on and I knew I'd have to be back to open the bar in less than an hour? Whatever, I felt very nervous suddenly. I checked the drawer again. Still no card. Then I remembered: when I'd gone to the C&C the previous week I'd been wearing my leather jacket – probably the card was still in one of the pockets. My jacket was upstairs.

Muriel would be down in the cellar checking the mixers and empties before the delivery that afternoon; Sylvia, our maid/waitress/receptionist would be in the kitchen helping to get the lunches ready. The building seemed very empty as I hurried up the carpeted stair, along the corridor and walked straight in through the door marked PRIVATE.

It took me several seconds to take in what I could see happening right in front of my very eyes.

Without saying a word I turned and came out the room. Back along the corridor, down the stairs, through the bar and I was in the car again. I drove out the small carpark, then I was at the top of the hill, then at the bridge. That's when I realised I could hardly see the road anymore. I pulled into the lay-by, switched off the engine, and sat.

I wasn't thinking about what I'd seen. I just sat, period. Nothing else. It took all my strength simply to remain there – not remembering, not thinking. Every time I reached to switch on the ignition my hand touched the key, then seemed to hesitate, and stop.

Eventually, of course, I did start the car and drive off. I went to the C&C, filled my pallet with cigarettes, crisps, matches, peanuts. When I reached the checkout I told them I'd lost my card and filled out the appropriate forms. Once back at the hotel, I parked, unloaded, and opened up the bar only thirty minutes late.

Sailor has just asked me what England need to get through to the next round and my voice tells him while my hand lifts his glass to give the bar a wipe. Being English I'll never be quite accepted here.

The service door has opened. It's Muriel.

Within seconds I've come out from behind the bar to collect glasses, wipe tables, chat with customers, anything.

I haven't spoken to her since that morning. During my lunch break she came to me in tears, with explanations and entreaties. Later, in the upstairs corridor, she got down on her knees, threw her arms around my legs and begged. She was willing to do anything, she said, to promise anything. I managed to get myself free without my hands touching her. That night I moved into one of the guest bedrooms where I locked the door, watched TV with headphones on and ignored everything else.

The fact is – I don't know what to do. Just as when I stood in the doorway and saw her, and didn't know what to say. Like I was in shock. Other men might have shouted, strutted and screamed, dragged her by the hair, or else tried to be reasonable, to be understanding, forgiving – set about talking things through. Some men might even have regarded her behaviour as a cry for help. Some might have been turned on. I'm not like any of these, it seems; and the question I'm left with is: what am I like?

What am I like? This is a question that's never come up before. Do I know the answer? The truth is that I haven't the slightest idea. Take the worst-case scenario: if she'd become furious with me – all acid-tongue and stabbing eyes – then at least I could have reacted. But she didn't, she's almost in shock as well. Her admission of helplessness is probably what's holding her together, that and a growing contempt for me.

'You'll be giving us a round on the house if we get through tonight?' Sailor calls over to me from where he and Slow Todd are seated waiting for the game to start. They're gazing blankly up at the TV on its special shelf high in the corner, pints in their hands and more pints on the table in front of them.

'If England qualify then I might,' I hear myself making a joke of it. We both laugh, though exactly what the joke is I'm not quite sure. Unless it's all the blue-painted faces, the tartan bunnets and the frantic goodwill.

I've a stack of glasses-within-glasses cradled in one arm. I should return to the bar and rinse them. It'll be kick-off in a few minutes and fresh glasses'll be needed soon enough. Instead, I head for the back door, and out into the yard.

I place the stack of glasses on the ground next to the kitchen door. It's a perfect summer's evening, the air warm and still and the village utterly silent. Everyone's getting ready for the game, even old ladies will be tuned in hoping Scotland manages to achieve something for once. There are only a couple of cars in the carpark besides ours, most people will have walked. It's going to be a long night.

The birds come from all over the world, parakeets from Africa, Egyptian reed warblers, Indian mynah birds – they're a great attraction for the customers. I've been collecting them for years, since long before we came up here and took over the hotel. It's a big enough cage, ten feet high and the size of a generous double bedroom, there's a living tree I keep trimmed for them to perch on. After a long night behind the bar I like to spend a calming last quarter of an hour in their company, making sure to lock their door when I leave. If they escaped they would never survive.

That roar coming from inside probably means the game has started. The place is bursting at the seams, standing room only – dozens of them cheering themselves tartan. Business will be up fifty per cent if they win, a hundred per cent if they lose – the Scots are generous in grief.

As I put the key into the small lock there's a sudden fluttering of wings, a hopping up and down along the branches. One of the budgies calls out, in its tinny speaker-sound of a voice, *'itsmichael, itsmichael'*, a phrase I taught it last summer. I latch the door behind me and take up my usual position in the centre of the cage with my arms outstretched. Within seconds several of them have flitted over to settle on my shoulders, my head, my open hands. When I close my eyes all I can sense is their almost weightless presence.

Another roar from the bar – how clumsy and earthbound men and women seem, compared to these aerial flutterings around me. I open my eyes and notice that the back door is now wide open, a broad slash of electric glare in the evening light. Muriel's standing in the doorway.

I shouldn't be out here. I have a business to run, customers to serve. I give my arms and shoulders a quick shake, and with a scuffling of wings, the odd screech and caw, the birds rise up to return to their usual perches. Moments later, having picked up my stack of glasses, I find myself face-to-face with Muriel.

'Michael, please, can't we just—'

I push past her into the clamour of the bar.

It's nearly 2 a.m.: Scotland lost and the bar's been in a relish of mourning for the last four hours. They've sung their songs, waved their little flags, shed tears some of them, and gradually eased themselves comfortably back into the familiarity of defeat. A few seconds ago, Slow Todd in a moment of rare eloquence announced to no one in particular:

'Naebody kens us like oorsels – and that's the making o us.'

'Get the man a pint.' Sailor's put a tenner down into a beer puddle on the counter, 'And one for me, and one for yersel.'

I pour two pints and pick up the sodden note.

'Yersel an all, Michael.'

At the other end of the bar Muriel's pouring someone a whisky.

She looks tired, exhausted. There are no winners around here, none that I can see anyway.

'A pint for yersel, mind,' he repeats.

I hear myself thanking him, then ring up the till and give him his change.

At long last the door's closed and bolted shut. With the TV off and the bar empty, the scene of glorious nationhood in full flood has returned to its usual state – a late night mess of trampled food, cigarette ends and crumpled crisp bags, of tables littered with spilling-over ashtrays, dirty glasses and empty bottles. Someone's left his 'tartan jimmy' hat on one of the seats, a Scottish flag droops half-unrolled from the windowsill.

I'm in the middle of stacking glasses for washing when I find myself wondering whether or not I locked the birds' cage earlier.

It feels chilly outside now; a clear sky of stars and a half-moon. No movement comes from the cage, not a sound. I was right to be concerned: the wire door isn't locked, not even latched, just pushed to – luckily there's no wind to blow it wide open. I'm about to pull it shut and lock it when I hear something in the far corner. A cat? One from Dailly's farm maybe, they're half-wild and go prowling the village and fields at night.

As I step inside I sense the birds' sudden agitation. Abruptly they start zigzagging about the cage. Wildcats are dangerous, they can bite and claw – half-wild cats? I hope it'll make a run for the door which I've now propped open slightly to let it escape.

Then I catch sight of…not a wildcat, but Muriel.

I'm furious: 'What the hell are *you* doing in here?'

All I can see is the outline of her head and shoulders, her fair hair catching what little light there is. I give her several seconds, but she doesn't reply.

I take a step towards her.

'I said, what are *you* doing here?' I'm almost shouting. But why the hell shouldn't I shout? All evening I've had to put up with other people shouting – shouting and roaring, and yelling their heads off.

Still no reply.

'Were you planning to stay in here all night? Because if you are, I'll just lock the door and leave you to it.'

I make as if to turn away, but when she still doesn't say anything I stop again:

'Well?'

Her face, the shadow of her mouth, her eyes, her fair hair are all becoming clearer in the moonlight.

'Look, Muriel, the door wasn't closed properly. These birds get out, and it's as good as killing them.'

'You're killing *me*.'

For several seconds I'm so surprised at what she's said I stand stock-still. I can't move, I can't speak. I can't seem to breathe hardly. Then, almost as if a switch has been thrown inside me, I turn towards the cage door.

Next thing, she's pulling me back, one hand dragging at my shirt, the other tugging my hair:

'Don't run away, you bastard.'

I grab for the wire-netting and hold on.

'You fucking selfish bastard.' She's yanking my hair so hard I cry out in pain:

'Let go, you bitch!'

At once the birds set up a frenzy of screeches and screams. To my left '*itsmichael, itsmichael*' begins repeating like a broken record. In our tussle the door's swung open a little wider.

I manage to twist my head round to face her but she won't let go. We start kicking each other, shoving and grabbing. Around us the birds are going crazy, diving, rising, wheeling in panic. Trying to force each other into the dirt; we howl and rage at the tops of our voices. Next second the two of us are on the floor of the cage rolling around in a mess of sawdust, earth, birdshit, feathers. Finally, we stop: our faces only inches apart.

Just then one of the birds, an Australian galah, steps lightly past where we're lying and continues towards the gap in the doorway. It pauses there for a moment to give its wings a preparatory stretch, then lifts itself into the air, soars up, and finally disappears into the darkness. Now that we have stopped fighting, the whole cage has become very quiet again, no screeches any more, no high-pitched calls.

The galah is followed by a South American weaver-bird that drifts in one perfectly unbroken arch from its branch straight out through the doorway, its whiteness becoming fainter and fainter, and finally dissolving to nothing.

I struggle to my feet: 'They'll die out there; they need looked after, they need—'

I pull the door shut and latch it.

Muriel's standing beside me. 'Have most of them gone?'

I don't answer her.

Her hand touches me on the arm. 'I'm sorry. I'm so very sorry.'

I manage to say: 'So you fucking well should be.' I want to be angry with her, as angry as I was before. 'So you fucking well should be, Muriel.' But my words seem to have no strength any more, no meaning.

Again she touches me on the arm, this time letting her hand remain there. I feel her warmth reaching me through the thin cotton.

The birds...I want to say, *The birds are...they are all that...For years I've looked after them, I've done everything I can to*...

But no words come. No tears come either, and no anger.

'Listen, Michael, when you saw me then, I was...'

I put my fingers to her lips to silence her. There are feathers tangled in her hair and a smear of birdshit down her cheek. Would her explanation help me understand anything? Would my forgiveness make our world right again? If I picked the feathers out of her hair, wiped the birdshit from her face, kissed her and said that I loved her – would it really change anything?

'It's late,' she says, then goes to step outside into the yard. I follow her. She shuts and locks the door firmly behind us.

The bar looks worse than ever, a mess that'll take hours to clear up properly.

'What a complete shambles,' says Muriel, 'Let's leave it until tomorrow. We can get up early.'

'But…' I begin to protest. Then I shrug my shoulders. She's right. Of course she is. We have tomorrow – just like we had today, yesterday and each one of the terrible days before that. If we wish it, we can have them all.

I switch off the light and follow her upstairs.

Sailor and his mother

Sailor's mother straightened up too suddenly from bending over the sink – and immediately the green kitchen walls buckled in and out, the floor ribbed to waves that all but knocked the feet from under her. She grabbed the rim of the stainless steel sink. That bastarding son of hers should have been up long past. The battery wall-clock, 'A Present from Ayr Where There's All the Time in the World', showed ten-thirty. Him and his sore head should have been down an hour ago. She'd knocked earlier like he'd asked, and waited to hear the first rush of water in the pipes and the *thud-thud* of his size-twelves on the stairs. Now his tea was cold and slicked over – a waste of good sugar. Call me at nine, he'd said. A job at Dyer's Cottage, he'd said.

One last try: she made her way up the stairs, pushed open his bedroom door and shouted in.

No response.

That window hadn't been opened in days: the bed-smell, the sweat, beer, fags and God only knows what else, about turning her stomach. The scrub of red hair, red beard, freckles and broken veins were all she could see of him. His shoulder stuck out from under the blanket. She shook it till he grunted. Then shook it again.

'Come on, Davey. It's half-ten.'

'Aye?'

'Ye lump, ye. Half-ten, I'm telling ye.'

'Aye.'

More like a breathing out between his teeth than speaking. He'd be going back to sleep any second.

'You were to be at Dyer's Cottage an hour past. Man'll be waiting.'

'Aye, I'll be down.'

'You'd better.'

Sailor's mother stood up from leaning over the bed and again felt her legs all but giving way. She took good hold of the wooden headboard and stayed where she was. The curtains were hanging half-open – outside she could see what looked like a dozen fields slithering together into a heap of yellows and greens, then separating again into one field each of rape and grass; Douglas Brae had a dozen tops to it, and all of them trembling, keeping time with the vein pulsing at the side of her head.

When the room finally settled down to its usual midden of clothes on the floor, the oiled saw leaning against the wall, the rabbit snares, the netting and waders, and the old shotgun next to the wardrobe, she glared down at her son – but that lump of nigh-on-fifty-years-of-running-after had already gone back to snoring wetly on its pillow. Another job lost.

Sailor had been thirty-four when he'd returned home after ten years in the Merchant Navy. No letter, no phone call to let them know he'd be arriving. Not a word – their only warning was the sound of someone barging his way into their front lobby.

'Whae the hell's that?' her old man had called out above the whooping red Indians and gunshots of the western he was watching at near full-volume – not that he'd be expecting anybody much; the minister, say. Anybody else would come to the back door. Sailor's mother had nearly dropped her cup with the shock as the living-room door opened with no sound of a greeting coming through first.

And there he'd stood: blue jeans, white vest, brown leather jacket and a tan to match. All five foot ten of him looking pleased and awkward as he stood half in the room and half out. Beard like a hedge needing seen to.

'You're back then?' A jerk of the head from her old man who'd no intention of getting to his feet, that was clear.

'Davey, son!'

She'd rushed over, holding him tighter than she'd done since he was a boy, and trying not to cry; behind her the Indians were still whooping, their ponies' hooves still hammering and thundering round the wagon train. It had been eight-thirty when he'd come in the door; a warm summer's evening with daylight still so clear it made winter seem impossible.

Through in the kitchen she'd given him the biggest fry-up ever while her old man sat at his end of the table with a cup of tea. For the next hour they heard about China, Madagascar, the Pacific, so large he'd forgotten what dry land looked like, and the north coast of Greenland and beyond, where the creak and muffled boom of the ice-floes drifting past sounded like the ship was breaking up.

Then the two of them went off to the pub, leaving her to make a start on Davey's clothes. There'd been a lock-in in his honour, her old man boasted when they came staggering back, Davey loud-voicing his plans ahead as he came in the door – plans about renting the low field from Stuart, about buying some sheep, hens, bees, pigs, a boat and night-lines for the loch, a van and tools for repair work. Slow Todd and Cammie trooped in clutching a carry-out so big it needed the pair of them. A late night, and it was she who had to speak up about their beds with the daylight already well started behind the closed curtains and the living-room a mess of men and smoke and crushed cans. They'd woken Todd, and

Cammie said he'd see him home. Davey had managed himself up the stairs, second try.

Back in the kitchen Sailor's mother got on with the labelling: two dozen honey, two dozen jam. Not a lot, but better than nothing. The honey was for selling, the jam they'd have on bread, rolls, scones, toast, in puddings and cakes till it got used. Five jars more and she'd put on the kettle so it would be boiled in time for her finishing.

She was on her third-last label that just wouldn't stick straight but seemed to jerk in her hands each time she pressed it onto the glass, when she heard a knock at the front door. The jar nearly jumped out of her hand – which would've meant £1.50 turned to stickiness and smashed glass on the floor – but she managed, slow-motion and double-handed, to place it on the formica worktop. She held her breath and listened, and waited. Front door was where the grief came in: Social Security, police, anything official, anyone after somebody or something – usually that bastarding waste of space upstairs in its bed.

Another knock. She was standing next to the low electric humming from the Ayr clock, a never-ending grumble she'd learnt to put up with – she'd always wanted an old-fashioned wind-up one, the sort that struck out every tick with a clear back-and-forward swing of its pendulum. She'd wanted, so she never got. Who did? It was nearly eleven, too late for the post. There were footsteps on the side path: the bad news was coming round to the back.

A blur of tallness was suddenly darkening the pebbled-glass of the kitchen door, a knuckle rapping the woodwork. Whoever it was would be trying to peer in soon enough: she hadn't the strength to get herself through into the sitting-room and out of sight. She went to the door.

'Sorry to bother you, but is this where *Sailor* lives?'

Waxed jacket, green cords and anxious-looking – the man from Dyer's Cottage, it had to be.

'He sleeps here.'

'Oh?'

On second glance, the waxed jacket looked short in the arms and the cords concertina-ed below the knees: either very well off, or no better than he should be.

'Let you down, has he?'

'I was expecting him two hours ago. Supposed to be bricking up a loose bit of wall. Getting kind of urgent. I'm in the old place beyond the farm.' The man pointed up the road with a hand that was obviously no working hand, and never had been.

At that moment Sailor's mother heard the water in the pipes and knew the *thud-thud* would be coming after.

'Why don't you come in? He's just getting himself ready.'

Fifteen minutes later the man from Edinburgh who'd bought Dyer's Cottage to do up for weekends, had also bought two jars of honey and been given two of raspberry jam 'for goodwill'. The pleasure of his new purchases notwithstanding, he couldn't stop thinking about the back wall of his cottage: he could picture the large stones that had loosened overnight and now rocked at a touch like milk-teeth. It had rained heavily all the previous day so he'd not been surprised when Sailor hadn't appeared. Today though, with the drier weather, some of the larger stones were all but rolling free; here and there the wall above them was cracking, threatening to give way. The man who'd bought Dyer's Cottage sat drinking tea he didn't want while imagining the uninterrupted view there would soon be from his garden straight into his kitchen, bathroom and bedroom when the back wall finally collapsed. Which might very well be happening at that precise moment. Meanwhile he was being kept perched on the edge of a kitchen chair, gripping the edge of a kitchen table, drinking tea and listening to Sailor's mother telling him, at considerable length, what a lazy so-and-so her son was. The man was aye letting folk down, she was saying, and it was a wonder folk kept asking him.

'If only Davey'd met a good girl who'd have made something of him, but what lass is going to stop in the village? What's she to stop for? It's brains or bairns nowadays; they've either left the place for something better or stayed and got themselves hitched by eighteen. "Sailor" they might call him, but he's missed that particular boat long since.'

The man from Edinburgh couldn't remain in his seat a second longer. He picked up the Tesco bag with its dull-clinking jars and was about to make his apologies before leaving. But Sailor's mother was too quick for him and already heading towards the stairs:

'I'll take a stick to the good-for-nothing, you wait here.'

The three pounds she'd got for the honey was in her money tin and staying there. Once the lino was swept, it would be time to start cooking. The Dyer's Cottage man had gone, and so had another job. Davey was nowhere to be seen – he must have sneaked out the front door, the feckless lump. Would she give him yet another talking to when he got back from wherever, or just bang down his dinner and say nothing? What did it matter anyroad? She'd done this floor a thousand times, and here she was – still doing it. Trying to talk sense into that sack of stupidity was no different.

These days she seemed to sweep harder than ever, and the floor seemed dirtier than ever: bits of eggshell, onion skins, a tea bag, a hank of sheep's wool. The brush kept sticking in the corners, banging itself against the skirting-board like a live thing. As she lifted the metal dustpan for emptying, it clattered against the oven door. Her head swam and she staggered a couple of steps like she was going to faint. She put her free hand on the cooker to give herself a bit of ease. Yes, she'd save her breath; she'd wasted more than enough on that do-nothing disgrace who went around the village dressed like a burst bin-bag.

She placed the dustpan against a leg of one of the kitchen chairs to make brushing into it easier. 'Think someone'd invent longer handles,' she heard herself say out loud. 'But it won't be thon burst bin-bag, anyroad!' She laughed. That was her Davey and no mistake. The more she thought of him looking like that the more she laughed.

She was still laughing when she straightened up after the last of the sweeping. There was another rush of dizziness. She reached for the kitchen table to steady herself. But there was no table any more. No table, and no chairs, no worktop, no cooker. Instead, it seemed to Sailor's mother that her whole kitchen had turned into an almost blinding light, and she'd only to reach out her hand to grasp hold of the brightness spread all around her...

Sailor'd had a good day. After a late lie-in he'd skipped breakfast, slipped out the front door to keep well clear of his mother and the Dyer's Cottage man, and gone round to Todd's for a hair of the dog. Then the two of them had checked the rabbit snares he'd set the day before: a brace of full-grown ones apiece. Next, down to the nets in the bridge pool: three salmon and a trout. They'd built a fire in Corbie Wood, skinned, gutted and cooked one of the rabbits while finishing off Todd's bottle. Todd was a good man to pass the day with – not a great talker. Sailor lay in the grass by the fire staring up into the afternoon sky. His ten years away were more and more like memories of someone else's life, not his. Whenever he'd gone ashore with the others after weeks on end at sea, it had been a mad scramble to get drunk and laid. All he could remember now were windowless rooms and beds with curtains pinned up round them, that and being glad to get back onboard afterwards. Since returning home he'd never left the village, nor wanted to.

Once the fire had burnt itself down to red and grey ash, he and

Todd had gone to the hotel to sell the fish and rabbits. Then they'd had themselves a really good night.

It was long after eleven when Sailor tacked his way home down the middle of the empty main street. There was no light in the cottage. No sense in waking up his mother by clattering all the way through the kitchen and sitting-room, so he went straight in through the front. He closed the door behind him and locked it – she must have forgotten – then began to haul himself up the stairs to bed.

By tomorrow's breakfast the job of fixing the back wall at Dyer's Cottage would be ancient history: he'd tell his mother he was going to spend the morning digging potatoes and promise to bring her back a good sackful. Fresh lifted, they'd be at their best. Sailor knew she loved them like that.

The man called Lockerbie

Every day's become a stay of execution. Check the red numbers on my bedside clock: get up/get washed/get dressed/have breakfast. Check the red numbers again, and glance outside. So far so good.

So far so good, I tell myself.

This is how the damned keep going. We've ceased to read our futures in the letter that doesn't arrive, the phone that doesn't ring, the promise that's not kept. We've ceased to wait for an answer to our prayers. We've ceased to pray, except as a gesture of defiance. We pray to find the strength for anger, for hatred even. Corrosion seeps into our lives, corrosion tasting of tears, sleeplessness and bitten-back rage.

So far so good, I tell myself as I hurry down Waverley Steps into the station. Fifteen minutes and I'll be safe: my uniform, my swivel-seat, my ticket machine, my stretch of counter. There are no windows in the Travel Centre, behind me is a blank wall and straight ahead the never-ending queue which gets its tail nipped off by the electronic entry-door hissing shut. From the moment I sit down my day's taken care of – dates and destinations/routes and prices/credit cards, debit cards, cheque books, cash. Eight hours that are as good as already over, eight hours well spent.

At ten-twenty there's an American:

'Lockerbie, please, two returns.'

Most likely he's a relative of someone killed on Flight 103. Almost certainly, in fact.

I tap out the computer code. While the tickets are being printed, I remark:

'That's my name.'

'Sorry?'

'I said, that's my name – *Lockerbie*.'

'Well, fancy that!' he replies, though it's obvious he doesn't care in the slightest. He takes the tickets and his change and walks away without a backward glance. Fair enough.

It isn't true, of course, about my name. But sometimes I pretend. People usually just nod, thinking I'm being friendly.

Two hours later, same again: 'Lockerbie, please.'

Another American, a woman. Well-preserved for sixty. Dyed candyfloss for hair.

'A ticket for Lockerbie, please. I'm in a hurry.'

I tap out the code, take her twenty-pound note. 'You realise the next Lockerbie train's not till three o'clock.'

'But the Birmingham one...?'

'Doesn't stop at Lockerbie, I'm afraid. Haymarket, Carlisle and stations south only. Three o'clock's your next one.'

'Oh.' She takes her change and the ticket.

'I should know,' I smile at her. 'I'm called Lockerbie myself.'

She doesn't smile back. 'Three o'clock you say?'

'Yes, madam.'

'Thank you.'

According to an article I once read, one out of three American women has had plastic surgery. Noses, breasts, hips, lips, face-lifts or whatever. Candyfloss certainly looked like she could afford it. That kind of money. My own fiscal policy's simplicity itself: pay the rent, get rid of the rest and start the new month with nothing carried over. Till I moved into the city I used to be a dedicated saver. Jobs after school, at weekends, during the holidays. Saying no to drugs, no to chocolate, no to a second can of lager, no to fags. I saved and saved. I wanted a set of wheels. Not just another shagging-wagon but something elegant, with style and speed. Leather seats, polished wood, electric windows – that kind of style. That kind of money.

What was I wanting for Christmas? my dad asked me one evening.

Cash, I said, towards a second-hand Jag.

He leant across the kitchen table: *Cost a bomb, that will.*

Not his last words to me, but I don't remember any of the others.

Twelve fifty-five: the THIS COUNTER IS CLOSED sign gets placed on my section. An hour for lunch. An hour to get through. Out the swivel-seat, off with the uniform, on with the outdoor jacket. Then head up the Waverley Steps and across Princes Street to the Café Royal, to my soup, pie and pint.

'You're the man called Lockerbie, aren't you?'

It's the American candyfloss again. Old enough to be my mother, my grandmother even. Yellow-blonde, with painted-on eyebrows, bright red lips. A good sixty.

'Yes,' I nod politely. 'Sorry about your train.'

'Well…' She shrugs, and takes a sip of what looks like gin and tonic. 'Been putting it off long enough – a few hours more don't signify, I guess.'

I nod and say, 'Hmmm… I suppose not.' Luckily my soup and pie arrive. Well-timed.

I don't mind her being here, but I'd have preferred to be sitting with Frank or Toby. When we're not talking work-talk Toby goes on about football and Frank goes on about saving the environment.

When it's my turn, I go on either about the break-up of British Rail, or else the rail network before Dr Beeching. Yesterday, Frank was telling us that before the reign of Henry VIII, you could walk from John O'Groats to Land's End, treetop to treetop, your feet never touching the ground – I pointed out that before Beeching's cuts you could have made exactly the same journey by train and still not touched the ground. *Branch*-lines? he asked. He was joking, of course. Conversation helps lunchtimes to pass.

I lift my pint to the American lady and say 'Cheers!'

She *Cheers!* me back. 'Nice bar.'

'That's why we're both here!'

A nod from each of us this time. Then, to my surprise, we laugh. Without even meaning to. No reason. None, anyway, that I can see.

Five minutes later she's got herself some soup and a pie of her own, and another gin and tonic.

'Well, Mr Lockerbie, have you been there?' She pauses. 'I mean, to Lockerbie?'

'No.' My immediate response, then I add: 'Tell a lie – yes, I suppose I have. Pass through it sometimes on the way to Birmingham and the balmy south!'

She's a pleasant, friendly woman. I can say whatever I want to her and she'll believe me. Not that I'd abuse her trust, of course, and start telling her about that night out on the hillside above the town, picking up the metal bits, the plastic bits, the jackets and overcoats, the holdalls and suitcases, the trays and blankets, the body parts and what might have been body parts...It would only upset her.

After a few seconds she says, 'Coincidence you having the same name and all.' But she's not interrogating me, just commenting.

Whether it's because of her bright red lips or me wondering about how soon I'll need to leave the pub to get back in good time to my uniform and swivel-seat, I find myself picturing the red numbers on my alarm clock – the countdown that's begun every single morning of my life in Edinburgh and that's going on even at this very moment.

'Yeah, a real laugh.'

'I'm sorry. I don't mean to be insensitive.'

'No, you're right. If I did come from Lockerbie – it *would* be a real laugh.' I'm grinning now. 'Imagine telling people my name: Bill Lockerbie, from Lockerbie, I'd say. A real laugh. That's what I'd have to say: I'm Bill Lockerbie from Lockerbie.'

Nearby a few people have stopped talking and are glancing over, staring at me. I take a good pull at my beer and keep the eyes down until I hear the general chit-chat's go back to normal again.

She's said something and is holding out her hand.

I lean towards her. 'Sorry, I didn't quite catch…'

'My name's Betsy. Betsy Hillmeyer.'

'Pleased to meet you.' We shake. 'Fancy another then, Betsy?'

'Why not? Thank you.' She gets to her feet. 'If you'll excuse me.'

I direct her to the toilets, and then order. The bar's thinning out now that the 12.30–1.30 lunch breaks have headed back to work. Betsy and our drinks arrive at the same time.

'Been in Scotland long?' I ask her.

'Flew into Prestwick first thing this morning. Back home on Monday. Kind of spur-of-the-moment, whirlwind trip. Been putting it off like I said. Now, bang! here I am. Cheers!'

It looks like the G&Ts are getting to her.

'Funny my bumping into you – Mr Bill Lockerbie and all!' She taps the back of my hand, not flirtatiously or anything, just good-humouredly.

'Well, there's plenty more of us, you'll meet them when you

get there!' I'm making a joke, I think. I laugh anyway and so does she. 'The three o'clock's a direct train. Waverley, then Haymarket three minutes later, and next stop's Lockerbie. No changes.' I stop myself from going on about the complicated shunting there used to be at Carstairs, how the Edinburgh train had to wait before joining up with the one from Glasgow, and all the rest of it – she wouldn't be interested. 'About an hour, if it's on time.'

'If it's on time,' she repeats in a slurry kind of voice.

I tell her: 'Speaking of which, it's time I was off.'

But here she is, wanting to get me one back.

'Someone's got to keep the trains of Britain running!' I joke, and finish my pint.

'Okay, another time.' She's turned abruptly and ordered herself another gin. A trifle miffed, perhaps.

Politeness speaks up: 'That's kind of you, Betsy. Okay, a whisky, please. But I'll need to be quick. I'm sorry.'

She's relaxed again and calls the barman. 'Cancel that gin. A special order's coming up.' Then she turns to me: 'What's the best single malt?'

Problem is – I rarely drink spirits and wouldn't know a malt from a blend, except for the price. I glance along the shelf of bottles above the mirror.

'Glen Islay's a good one.'

The barman gives a snobby kind of shrug. Betsy meets my eye.

I add, 'It's *my* favourite.'

'Let's make it doubles then, Bill. No, triples. For luck!' She pulls out her purse, waves a ten, then a twenty. 'This be enough?'

Next thing I know it's ten-past, then half-past. She's drunk now, and rapidly getting drunker. I'm late and rapidly getting even later. My glass is full again. By now the whisky's not just going to my head but seems to be going everywhere at once. A pleasing numbness made up of Betsy's friendliness, the old-fashioned counter with its brass fittings and varnished wood, the sunlight coming in through the large windows, the growing quiet around us. She's telling me about her life since Flight 103. She's remarried and taken on a grown-up son and daughter... 'Eighteen years. A lot can happen in eighteen years, can't it?'

I say yes.

Two-fifty, and we're struggling our way down the Waverley Steps, Betsy clutching my arm to steady herself. I'm carrying her suitcase. Some steps we seem to manage very quickly, too quickly almost, while we get stuck at others. I lead her to the right platform. Three minutes till her train's due to go. Suddenly she's started crying. We stand on the platform, her suitcase beside us, me holding her up and her with her head resting on my shoulder.

'Can't you tell them you're ill?' she mumbles into my jacket.

'What?'

'Tell them you're really ill, and come to Lockerbie with me. Separate rooms and everything. Please, Bill. I can pay. Mr Hillmeyer's a wealthy man.'

I raise my head from the swirl of hair and glance round. If one of the ticket inspectors recognises me... At least I'm not in uniform.

'Please, Bill. I don't think I can go. Not on my own. I thought I could, but...'

The guard's begun working his way up the platform, closing the carriage doors with a slam. He's getting nearer. At the head of the train Keith the porter, whose boast is that he's never carried anything but his own sandwiches, is chatting to the driver. I turn away. *Slam! Slam!* The door directly in front of us has been shut. Next to us a woman is waving goodbye to a tattooed man in the nearest compartment, a boy with an excited collie dog that's pulling him all over the place shouts through the window to his friend. Behind us there's the thump of taxis going over the speed-bump. The tannoy booms and crackles overhead like some god losing his voice.

'I must be a little drunk.' Betsy's stood back and picked up her suitcase. 'But if I have to manage, then I'll manage. I've come all the way over here, haven't I?'

Quickly I step forward and open the carriage door for her. She climbs in.

'Nice meeting you, Bill. Goodbye.'

'Goodbye.'

She touches the side of my face with her hand, and is gone.

Seconds later – it's not that I take a decision, more like I just stop thinking for a moment – I open the door and climb aboard.

In quick succession the about-to-depart warning is given, the doors lock and the train begins to move. The carriage is packed with men, women, children, babies; there are newspapers, books, bottles, food cartons, magazines, spare clothes scattered all over the seats and tables; suitcases block up the aisles, coat arms and scarves dangle from the racks...

What the hell am I doing here?

The train's entered the tunnel after Princes Street Gardens. And there's Betsy sitting halfway down the compartment next to a window. I'd recognise that candyfloss hair anywhere. Her face turned away from the other passengers, she's staring out at the darkness, dabbing her eyes with a tissue.

There's still time. I don't have to go up to her. I don't have to speak to her. In a couple of minutes I can get off at Haymarket, hop onto a return train, make some excuse and get back to my uniform, back to my swivel-seat, my ticket machine, my stretch of counter...

So far so good, I tell myself.

So far so good. The train's pulled into the station and shuddered to a halt. All I have to do is step out onto the platform and I'm safe again. Back to the red numbers, back to the letters that never come, to the phone that never rings, to the prayers that are more like screams. Back to this life of mine, this stay of execution.

Forty-five seconds will have to pass before the doors close again. I've started counting. And then? AND THEN? Ever since that terrible night not even the damned, it seems, know what's going to happen next. Nor how things must end.

Visiting the professor

Only in the car did McDowell realise how drunk the professor really was. Three attempts to click his seat belt, four to fit his key into the ignition. Getting on for midnight and with more snow looking likely, the twenty-mile drive to the professorial home started with a smack into the kerb and a bump up over the pavement. Finally, once they were heading down the empty street, the headlights were switched on.

Out of town there was plenty of road and Professor Dalziel soon had them drifting from side to side over the white markings. McDowell wondered how it was all going to end: getting killed he could cope with...

'Bitch of a road.' The professor's first words since leaving the restaurant carpark.

McDowell gave a nod but said nothing.

The professor was looking over at him: 'Bitch of a road, I said.'

'So it seems.'

A forty-five degree lurch to stay out of the ditch, and they were back on course: the white lines slithered under their lights, sometimes coming from the left, sometimes from the right. The man had started to keep his eyes on the road, at least. And to watch his speed, sort of: accelerate to fifty, hold steady for a half mile or so, begin slowing down till they were almost at a standstill, then stamp hard on the accelerator shooting them back up to fifty again. The dashboard lights turned the professor's face sea-green going on sick-green; he was sweating with concentration, his knuckles standing out bleached white like the fossils McDowell's drilling-crews sometimes came across. The twenty-mile road had become endless and would go on, it seemed, forever: the two of them were the first men on Earth, or else the very last.

The professor was staring straight ahead: 'My wife hasn't slept with me for five years.'

The man must have been too guttered to know just how guttered he really was. Apart from faxes and emails concerning the Research & Development programme funded by McDowell's firm, they hardly knew each other. Their business concluded, the professor had driven McDowell to the station, only to find the train to Edinburgh had been cancelled due to bad weather. Instead, the professor had phoned home and the two of them had gone for dinner. Up until that jarring intimacy a moment ago, their conversation had stuck to funding, to R&D, to minerals, mining and metal fatigue.

The abruptness of the professor's confession seemed to take them through the fifty-mph-max cycle of boom-and-bust, and they began picking up speed.

'Divans, then separate rooms. We're still speaking, you understand, Peter, but I'm a lodger in my own house and she's the landlady. With me?'

'Sorry to hear it.' What else could he say?

The next five minutes passed. There were no turnoffs, nothing to be seen of the surrounding country except hedges, a tree, another tree, now and again a darkened house. It started to snow.

'You can meet her. Meet Candice, I mean. She'll like that.'

The white flakes were rushing towards them thicker and faster, zigzags spraying across the windscreen. The effect reminded

McDowell of – what? An electrical storm perhaps, meteors, a shower of welding sparks, subatomic particles?

Finally, the professor thought to switch on his wipers: 'Bitch when the weather's like this.'

Without warning the car brakes suddenly, slides into a skid, slams into the kerb, then up. And jolts to a halt: half on the pavement, half on the road.

'Home sweet home,' comes the announcement.

They climb out into the cold and hunch their way head-down through the driving snow towards a two-storey house set back from the road. Here and there, areas of pebble-dash have been scabbed over with cement and left unpainted. The two of them huddle together on the porch.

'Bitch! Bitch! Bitch!' There seems to be trouble with the key.

With McDowell's help the door is opened.

'I told her to leave the light *on*!' The professor doesn't say this quietly. He fumbles for the switch.

They're in a large, panelled hall that clearly doubles as an open-plan living-room, with two couches facing each other in front of an empty grate. The flooring's polished wood, straight ahead there's a staircase and various doorways to the side.

'Something to drink?' His host walks towards one of the doors.

Drying off and getting straight into bed is all that McDowell's interested in. However, he is a guest.

'Coffee'd be fine, thanks…'

Through in the kitchen the professor's trying to fill a kettle. He shouts above the rush of tap-water: 'Snow's wet, eh! My wife'll get you a towel.'

'No, it's okay. Really, I don't want to cause any—'

'No problem, Peter. She'd love to meet you.' Already he's come back into the hall. He's sobered up a bit, or seems to have.

McDowell draws attention to how late it is, adding that there's really no need to disturb her. 'I'm about dry already,' he explains, just stopping himself in time from grabbing the man's hand and sticking it into his hair with a *See?*

'D'you not want to meet my wife?'

'Yes, but—'

'Right then.' The professor strides over to the foot of the stairs: 'Candice! Candice!'

McDowell keeps pace with him, trying to point out that tomorrow morning might be better, that they'll see each other at breakfast…

'CANDICE! Mr McDowell's here. He wants to meet you.'

There's no response. The stairs lead up to a landing where there are three doors, all shut.

'She'll be down in a minute. Just getting herself ready.' The accompanying smile is obviously meant to reassure.

For several seconds the two of them stand side by side saying nothing.

Abruptly, taking aim at the first floor, the professor bellows: 'MR McDOWELL, I said! Remember him? He's come all the way from Edinburgh.'

Through in the kitchen the kettle's starting to boil.

As McDowell spoons some Nescafé into a mug taken from the drying rack, he hears the professor thumping his way up the staircase: 'McDOWELL! He's the man putting the research money into the Department, into this house…'

There's some milk in the fridge. He helps himself while listening to what sounds like the professor hammering at his wife's bedroom door. He goes to stand at the window and stares into the darkness where the snow's now falling even thicker. The outside world looks so very peaceful. For McDowell this is a moment of unexpected calm.

The shouting and banging upstairs has stopped. There are voices, the tread of footsteps on carpet, then on parquet flooring.

The professor's wife comes into the kitchen — she seems a good two inches taller and several years older than her husband. Not a particularly attractive-looking woman either, hair like an untrimmed hedgerow, a complexion like spoilt fruit; the padded yellow dressing-gown doesn't help.

She approaches, holding out her hand: 'Mr McDowell, how good of you to stop by. I hope Philip has been looking after you?'

They shake hands.

'Yes, thanks. I'm sorry to turn up so late like this, Mrs Dalziel. My train was cancelled and—'

'Call me Candice, please.' She turns to her husband hesitating in the doorway, 'Phil, why don't you get us some glasses and the single malt? You like Laphroaig, Mr McDowell?' A perfect-hostess smile.

'Yes, thank you. Call me Peter, please.'

'Well, Peter, we'll do our best to make you feel welcome.'

McDowell's seated on one couch, the professor and his wife on the other. Candice laughs. 'Looks like I've some catching up to do.'

For the next half-hour she keeps refilling McDowell's glass as well as her own. Whenever she crosses her legs she makes quite a show of repositioning the yellow-quilted dressing-gown afterwards. At his end of the couch the professor sits slumped forward, glass in hand, staring down at the stretch of fluffy red rug at his feet. His wife talks about having been brought up in Edinburgh. She and McDowell discuss restaurants, bars, galleries and theatres. She tells him how much she loves city life and city people. She's being flirtatious, but McDowell doesn't take it personally.

Finally the professor's had enough.

'Candice, go to bed.'

'But Phil, darling, I was in bed when you arrived. And asleep. I'm wide awake now.'

'Well, I'm not.'

'Then don't wait up. I'm sure Peter and I can finish off the Laphraoig without your help.'

The professor makes a clumsy snatch at the whisky bottle. He seems to have become very drunk all over again, and shouts: 'You've had enough!'

Candice glares back at him. 'You can say that again!'

The professor tries to get to his feet, but slips so he's half-kneeling on the floor. To steady himself he clutches at his wife's arm.

'Leave me – *alone*!' She wrenches herself free and stands up.

Better late than never, McDowell too gets to his feet. 'Time I was in bed.' He even manages a yawn.

Neither host nor hostess pay him any attention.

On his way to the stairs he can hear them laying into each other. 'You bitch!'... 'Fucking disgrace you are, Phil!'

Briefcase in hand, he starts making his way up to the landing in search of a bathroom and then his bed when he hears the professor calling after him. He keeps going. The professor calls up from the foot of the stairs. 'Sorry about that, Peter. Please don't think that—'

McDowell turns to face him: 'It doesn't matter. It's late. I'm very tired. Been a long day.' Is he being tactful, or forgiving even? He really doesn't care.

'Your room's on the left. Sleep well.'

They say goodnight. McDowell leans over the banister intending to call goodnight to Candice. But she seems to have vanished.

McDowell no longer sleeps well at any time, let alone in an unfamiliar bed. Two hours later he's still wide awake. He gets up. At least the snow seems to have stopped. He can make out the professor's car where it slewed to a standstill on the pavement. For a second or two he imagines leaving the house and driving back to Edinburgh – he'd seen the keys dropped on the hall table. Tempting, certainly.

Not only is he wide awake, but he's thirsty. Not used to drinking, especially neat whisky. Having pulled on his clothes, he tiptoes out to the landing, past the other closed doors and then, step by step, he descends into the complete darkness and stillness of downstairs.

Only when he's reached the kitchen and shut the door behind him, does he switch on a light. He goes over to the fridge and pours himself some milk. From where he's now seated at the breakfast bar the windowpane appears as a sheet of black glass showing his reflection. If someone were looking in, what would they see? he wonders. A man who'd got back late having been delayed by the bad weather, or who's been working late, or who's still up because his wife or child isn't well… ? Whatever, seeing him now, they'd think he was a man in his own home, safe and secure…

With a start McDowell turns round.

Candice is standing in the kitchen doorway. 'Sorry, Peter, I didn't mean to startle you. I said, I'm glad to see you're making yourself at home.'

'*At home*? I don't understand. I mean—' He's flustered, like someone caught in the act. 'I just helped myself. I hope you don't mind.'

'Not at all.' She smiles.

'I woke up very thirsty suddenly.'

She seems to pause for a moment, then half-laughs. 'Maybe I'll join you.' She comes across to sit next to him.

McDowell takes another sip of milk.

As she leans forward, she holds her dressing-gown tightly closed. 'Can I be blunt with you?'

'Of course.' He nods and hopes he's not going to be treated to her side of the marriage story.

'Well, Peter, it's your Research & Development money that keeps my husband's department afloat – did you know that?'

'No, I'd no idea. Your husband never said.'

'No research money, no department, and no us. Phil is too much of a gentleman and a scholar to tell you. So *I'm* telling you.' She pauses, then looks him directly in the face. 'Don't hold last night's little episode against him, please. He's very on edge.'

'It's forgotten.'

'*He* won't have forgotten.'

'Tell him there's no problem—'

'He'll bring it up and keep bringing it up. He'll crawl, he'll beg.'

McDowell pretends to laugh.

'*Beg*.' She turns away as if spitting out the word. 'Beg, until it makes me feel like stamping on him to shut his mouth.'

The woman's fingernails, he notices, are beautifully cared for – not talon-long but smoothed to a perfect curve with a mother-of-pearl sheen turning palest blue as they catch the light. An unattractive woman who's found something about herself to cherish.

To his surprise, after a short, awkward pause he hears himself saying, 'One thing, Candice, you do have lovely hands.'

With an abrupt movement she hides them from sight in her lap while mumbling what sounds like, 'Thanks.'

There was a time when McDowell would have now gone on to play the gallant with this unattractive woman, taking her hand, patting it, saying that she needn't worry, that the department will continue to get its money. He would have smiled and probably sat for a while longer flirting innocently with her before returning upstairs, he to his room and she to hers.

Instead, he goes over to rinse his glass under the tap.

As he lets the water run, he hears Candice's chair being pushed back. He forces himself to stare into the night – at the rectangle of brightness, at his shadow falling across the unmarked snow, the total stillness.

A few steps, and now she's right behind him. And…and all at once McDowell is gripped by an overwhelming certainty – the certainty of having at last arrived in a distant and strangely familiar world. He is utterly stranded and alone, and yet no longer feels afraid. How long has he been travelling to reach here – the last few terrible months, the years before that, his whole life? If there is a name for this shunned place, he has yet to discover it.

'Peter?' Candice is standing very close.

He doesn't move.

What can she be hoping for? If McDowell thought he had anything to offer her, he would gladly open wide his arms to give whatever treasures this world contains – from the darkness that surrounds it, to the light buried and burning at its core…

Only when he is quite certain the professor's wife has left the kitchen and gone back upstairs, does McDowell turn round.

Before him is the empty kitchen, the living-room with the couches where the three of them sat drinking together, the hall, the staircase leading to his bedroom upstairs…Beyond these lies the rest of this new world, stretching in all directions and waiting to be explored – the darkness, the snow-covered road, the railway that will take him back to the city, back to the flat where he now lives, to his suite of offices in the New Town, and to the day ahead.

He has only to endure, he tells himself. Endure. It will be bearable. Like everything else in this unnamed place, it will be bearable.

Taking Jazza's place

The Student Accommodation Service had sent him to a top-floor flat in a stone tenement held together by scaffolding; it stood in a cul-de-sac of uncollected bin-bags, broken glass, dogshit and lack of sunlight. Not knowing Edinburgh, Simon had arrived there nearly forty minutes later than arranged. The stair lights made a buzzing noise, flickering off and on as he and his suitcases bumped their way up the three flights.

The guy who answered the door looked exactly like the kind of person his parents had warned him against: red-and-green hair, earrings, black leather waistcoat.

'Hi, you'll be taking Jazza's place then?' A friendly smile. 'Come in. I'm Danny, by the way.'

He was shown around the flat in less than two minutes. Danny, it seemed, had been waiting in for him.

'Here's the kitchen, and here's your shelf... That's your room down on the right – sharing with Colin who'll be back on Monday... That's my room. I share with Big Bozo, who'll be back on Monday as well... I'm off to my girlfriend's. Make the most of your quiet weekend, it'll be the last. See you.'

The front door closed. Danny had gone.

A moment later he was back again. 'Sorry to leave you like this...I forgot to say that the landlord lives opposite. He's called

Tommy. Any problems, you can speak to him. Only if it's desperate, mind…Nice man, for a landlord, but not a lot of help…You won't have any problems though. See you Monday.' The front door closed again. Danny's footsteps went hammering down the stairs. The street door banged.

Simon struggled down the corridor to his room on the right, his suitcases bumping against the wall. Monday. He was going to be all on his own until Monday. He'd get unpacked. He'd make himself a cup of tea. He'd feel better.

First thing, he opened the window to air the room while he did what he could to make himself feel at home. But which drawers were his, and which Colin's? Which parts of the wardrobe? There were clothes, books, computer disks, paper scattered everywhere. Both divans were unmade – one had a bare mattress and a sleeping-bag, the other sheets that glistened like fish-and-chip wrappings. Unfinished mugs of coffee, an open carton of milk and a half-eaten Chinese carry-out in its aluminium container stood on the chest of drawers. Squashed beer cans lay on the floor. Wherever he went he scrunched fried rice and noodles into the carpet. He found the hoover, then cleared a path between his bed and the door. Above the sleeping-bag – his bed, as the more temporary-looking? – there was a Shirley Manson poster.

Having tidied up the room as much as possible without making it seem like he owned the place, he went out to buy a Chinese carry-out for himself. He ate it watching the TV. This was the highlight of his first evening living away from home.

Newsnight had just finished when the telephone rang. It was a girl. A girl calling from a pub by the sound of it. Loud music, people talking and laughing in the background, people having a good time.

'Is Big Bozo there, please?'

'Sorry, he won't be back until Monday.'

More laughter, as if another girl had come to stand next to her, then: 'You must be the new guy that's moving into the flat. Taking over from Jazza?'

'Yes, that's me. I'm Simon '

'Oh well, be seeing you around, Simon. Have a good weekend. Bye.'

Over the next two days he answered the phone several times and explained that he was taking over from Jazza. He bought a half dozen cans of beer and two Chinese carry-outs and walked himself into the ground visiting The Royal Botanical Gardens, Chambers Street Museum, Princes Street and Edinburgh Castle. He called home twice, removed and reinstated Shirley Manson half a dozen times at least.

He'd just come in from the street after a Sunday evening stroll down Lothian Road along to Haymarket and back up again, when he nearly tripped over a large bundle of rags lying at the bottom of the stairs. The bundle of rags groaned.

It was an old man, his head nestling in the crook of his arm. Was he ill? A heart attack? Should he call a doctor? Get one of the neighbours? The man might be dying.

Simon was about to step over him to ring one of the ground-floor door bells when the bundle addressed him.

'Thanks, son. Took a wee tumble to massel, that's all. Had a bit of a night out.'

'Can I help?'

Ten minutes later he was still hauling the old man up the stairs. First floor, then the second, with the old man getting heavier at every step. Which door? Then they were continuing up to the top floor…This was his landlord? The old man's key was on a piece of string he pulled from his pocket. He unlocked the door.

'Come in, son.'

The hallway was pitch-dark.

'A wee disagreement wi the Electricity.'

The stench grabbed him by the back of the throat: paraffin,

cooking grease, unwashed clothes, a toilet somewhere nearby – and there were other smells he didn't recognise. The old man straightened up, having lit two candles that were stuck onto a square of cut-out lino.

'Ma chandelier. Let there be light, eh no! Have a seat. I was wanting to offer you a wee something for your kindness.'

'No, really. Thanks, but – '

'There's some whisky around here somewhere, to recover us after all them stairs.'

'No, thanks, I – '

The landlord held up his chandelier and peered at him closely for the first time.

'D'ye no drink, son?'

'I do, mostly beer though.'

'Right enough.'

The walls seemed bare apart from one which was covered with scraps of paper and had a pink bathroom cabinet nailed to it, the only cupboard. There was a mantelpiece, a boarded-up fireplace, two sagging armchairs, a low table covered with mugs, glasses, bottles, a half-empty packet of sugar, a coffee jar. In one of the corners a heap of old towels, curtains and rags seemed to serve as a bed – it looked like a dog basket, without the basket or the dog.

'Take it out of you these stairs, eh no?'

'Yes. Well, I'd better be – '

His landlord placed the chandelier on top of the cabinet. It had a mirror fixed to the front and Simon saw himself reflected there as a shadow against a darkened background. Time to leave, he thought. Time to say thanks for the offer of a drink, and goodbye.

His landlord was pointing to the bits of paper stuck to the wall: 'Ma collection. I call it The Tommy Baird Gallery of Scotland.'

There were pictures torn from newspapers, magazines; some of them faded and yellowed, some very recent. Cartoons, advertisements, the new parliament building, mountain scenes, lochs, oil rigs, politicians, footballers, film stars...

'When I see something I like, or that's really important, then I tear it out – so long as it's Scottish, mind – and add it to the gallery. A ruler to keep things neat. No bad, eh?'

Simon peered closer. 'The Forth Road Bridge, Edinburgh Castle, Dounray – '

'Clever boy!'

'Walter Scott Monument, Sean Connery—'

'*Sir* Sean Connery.'

'Oh. And there's Braveheart—'

'Brave-arse, more like. American trash, but ye hiv tae keep up wi the times. See that yin?'

Simon was handed the chandelier. 'Haud that, son. Ye're a bit steadier than me. Up a bit, an we'll see him better.' His landlord pointed to a grainy newspaper picture that had been repaired with sellotape. 'Ken him?'

Simon leant forward and stared.

'Haud it steady will ye.'

'Sorry.'

'John Maclean. The great John Maclean.' The old man had brought his face up very close – it was grey and red, like liver rolled in flour; the half-closed eyes had a startled look, like someone who'd been woken too soon. 'He had a dream. A Socialist Scotland. Didnae ken that, did ye?'

'No.'

'A dream.' Then his landlord turned away. 'Bloody dreamer!'

There was a moment's pause.

'You said you'd some beer, son?'

Knowing he was making a big mistake, but not knowing how not to make it, Simon went across the landing to his own flat and returned with two cans of lager. One can each, then he'd leave.

He was amazed how quickly the beer affected the old man,

who soon began slurring his words and rambling. Every so often he'd struggle to his feet and stagger across to examine his gallery. Simon always followed him, afraid he'd stumble and set the place on fire. The floor was littered with torn-up newspapers.

'Archie Gemmell, Argentina '78,' he might announce, then slump back down into his seat.

At one point his landlord suddenly turned to him. 'So, what do you do that's so fucking wonderful?'

'I'm just finishing this, then I'll disappear.' Simon smiled, trying to make a joke of it.

But the old man wasn't listening. He'd raised his arm as if for silence. 'No, don't tell me.' He was swaying back and forth in his seat. Then he leant across the space between them. 'A student!'

'Yes. First day's tomorrow.'

'A fucking student. Am I right or am I wrong?'

'Yes. But' – trying to get something of his own into the conversation – 'but what kind of student? Can you guess that?'

A long pause. Then: 'Can I guess what?'

'What kind of student?'

'Does it fucking matter?'

Next moment his landlord was on his feet, lurching from side to side in front of him and pointing a finger into his face. 'Does it really fucking matter what the fuck the likes of you are doing?'

'I think I'd better—'

'Aye, maybe ye had.' The old man had collapsed back into his seat. 'Sorry, son. That was out of order. I'm a bit tired, that's all. Nae offence, eh? G'night.' He finished speaking, slipped sideways and passed out – all in one continuous movement.

Simon sat and looked at his landlord until he was quite certain the old man was asleep, then tried to take the can of beer from his hand, but it was held too tightly. Should he blow out the candles? He did so – in case of fire. A split-second later he realised he should have waited: now he'd have to feel his way by touch through the darkness and the debris, all the way to the door.

For several moments he sat there in the pitch dark, grinding his teeth together as he gathered the very last of his strength. Then, with all the accumulated fury of his quiet weekend, he cursed his landlord snoring opposite, he cursed his absent flatmates, he cursed the Student Accommodation Service — but, most of all, he cursed that fucker Jazza.

The Sheriff and Susie and Swanny

First of all there's THE SHERIFF: five foot at most, cowboy hat, sheriff's star, holster belt and six-gun, making his way round and round the block, keeping to the same pavement, and shooting on sight anyone he thinks looks smart enough to get the joke. He's nearly sixty and still saving up for a set of spurs.

Then there's SUSIE, sixteen last birthday, and with her cheek slashed open. That night she'd been trapped in the lane, with the side wall of Replica-Antiques at her back and, facing her, the high railings of the student halls. Clutching onto the metal bars, she bled and screamed.

And lastly, SWANNY. Limping in and out of the dental laboratory at the corner of the street, with a perfect smile in his mouth and thirty-five years on his shoulders. Big Brother Barry owns the lab and owns him too – all of him, from his thinning hair and gentle eyes right down to his Poundstretcher trainers.

Susie

The dental laboratory with its painted-over windows used to be the local corner shop. The white paint stops short of the top to let in a couple of feet of natural light, and from where she lives on the third floor opposite, Susie often catches sight of the two men who work there, hunched over their bench. A few minutes ago she saw one of them straighten up, take off his lab coat, then disappear beyond the narrow strip of unpainted glass – only to reappear moments later in a padded red jacket, pick up a cardboard box, then vanish again. Next thing, he's outside on the pavement.

While watching him unlock the van door and climb in, she touches the gash running down her left cheek. Like an itch at the tips of her fingers, there's always the temptation to unpick the stitches, to press her face against the window and begin screaming even louder than she did that night in the lane. The screaming's all she remembers.

She'd been coming from Nancy's just across Causewayside. It wasn't even eight o'clock so she decided to take her daytime short cut through Newington Lane, a short, narrow passage not too badly lit, and with plenty of students going in and out of their halls of residence on the other side of the railings. She and Nancy had shared some cider and two giggly joints…Turning away from the window Susie clicks open her vanity mirror and examines the ten-rung ladder of see-through thread sewn into her skin. It's healing, just like the doctor said. Isn't that what she wants?

The Sheriff

It was The Sheriff who'd found her. He'd been taking his final mosey around town before hitting the hay. Drunks were the best: they usually saw the joke when he drew his six-gun, *bam-bammed* them, upended the barrels and blew away the smoke. Sometimes they'd shoot back or even ask him to come for a drink, but he'd learnt it was best to giddy-up a pretend horse, give them a 'Next time, partner!' and ride off into the nearest sunset.

That night, by the time he found the girl, he should already have been back in his room – Mr Dukes locked the hostel at eight on the dot and afterwards opened the door for no one.

He'd been short-cutting his way down the lane when someone came hightailing it towards him. Too fast for him to go for his gun – the sidewinder was raging mad and crazy, all at the same time, and knocked him to the ground like he wasn't there. Back on his feet again, his hat and gunbelt straightened, he'd gone up to the girl clinging to the railings. He was still a couple of steps away from her when she'd started screaming.

He'd given them all the description they needed: a no-good snake-eyes, a drifter most likely just passing through. It wasn't someone who'd bunked at Mr Dukes, he told them. Every day since, he's polished his badge and spun the chambers of his six-gun to check they're all loaded, except for the empty one where the hammer rests. He no longer calls out to strangers – he's trailing that saddletramp and keeping his eyes peeled.

Today he's on the bench outside the student halls and every few minutes practising how he'll call out the varmint. Again and again – standing tall, beating him to the draw, and making him eat dirt. Then he re-holsters. Sits down for a spell, bides his time. Glancing up and down the main street, watching the doorways, the upstairs windows, the roofs. A bunch of townsfolk have just walked past laughing and going 'Bang! Bang!' He ignores them, gets to his feet and starts blazing away at *him*, aiming at the critter's feet, screaming at him to dance, then shooting him down like a dog.

Swanny

The deliveries are Swanny's responsibility. Today he's off to Peffermill with a box of crown and implant samples. As always, ever since the girl who lives in that flat opposite was attacked, he's wearing a tie. A mark of respect? A gesture of reassurance? Proof that he's not the kind of man – the sort who goes around badly dressed and badly behaved – who'd ever harm a woman? He's not quite sure himself, but every morning, without even undoing the knot, he slides the paisley-patterned silk over his head like a noose to preserve the perfectly centred Windsor.

The smooth running of the van is his responsibility as well. Which makes today a bad day – because either the battery's flat, or the plugs are dirty or the electrics are fucked or the tank's been drained. Or all of them at once. If he keeps turning the ignition Big Brother Barry'll hear it and be out in no time, asking why the hell's he not left yet. Then he'll get a bollocking about what a dead weight he is, and useless. Big Brother Barry gets as mad at him now as when they were kids, madder even sometimes. Swanny feels himself already going into a cold sweat. He has no idea what to do, except he knows he can't keep sitting there any longer, staring out the windscreen at the empty street, and going nowhere.

Susie

This morning, like every morning since she was slashed, Susie had got her dad to check each room in their flat before he left for work, and to lock every window. Once both her parents had gone, she'd deadlocked the door, bolted it top and bottom, switched on all the lights – even though it meant having the bathroom extractor-fan churning away, but she's not going to risk switching it off. Even now as she stands at her bedroom window, she's afraid to go down the short corridor to the kitchen. Instead, she watches the mad sheriff having some kind of fit by the look of things down on his bench – every few seconds, though, she has to give her attention to any change in the sound of the extractor-fan, any faint creak of a door handle being turned, a door being opened, a floorboard being stood upon. Ever since that terrible night she knows that anything might happen at any moment. The scar that she checks every few minutes in her vanity mirror gives a kind of reassurance.

But now, from down in the street, comes the *retch-and-whine* noise of someone's car not starting. *Retch-and-whine, retch-and-whine.* It's the dental lab's transit. The driver, that limping apology of a man, is pressing himself forward in his seat as if that might help and is getting more defeated-looking by the second. He should ask someone to give his van a shove. At the moment the only person in sight is the mad sheriff – her saviour and knight in shining armour, she doesn't think. The crazy old man just stood there in the lane that night waving his toy pistols and shouting at anybody who came near her.

Swanny and The Sheriff

The transit's going nowhere, that's for sure. Big Brother Barry hasn't appeared yet, thank God – when he does, there'll be hell to pay. Swanny glances towards the lab doorway, then pockets the ignition key. Easing himself from behind the steering-wheel, he slides over to the passenger side, taking the cardboard box with him, and lets himself out onto the street. He pulls the door closed as quietly as he can, then locks it. No noise so far and no one the wiser. He'll slip down Blackwood Crescent and take a bus from outside The Wine Glass. With luck he can make Peffermill and back in well under an hour. By then Big Brother Barry'll be away for his lunch – giving him a chance to fix the van. His only chance.

The crazy cowboy's stepped off the pavement and is lurching across the street towards him. Christ, that's all he needs: the mad bastard'll soon be shouting and wanting him to go for his gun.

'No time for games today, old man. I'm busy,' he says.

From out of the corner of his eye he can see Big Brother Barry's shadow behind the window, moving in the direction of the lab door.

The cowboy's standing right next to him now.

'Not now, for Christ's sake!' He'll have to push his way past.

'I'm in a hurry.' The door of the dental lab'll open any moment. He has to get away.

The Sheriff has taken up his gunfighter's stance: jacket pushed back, hand above his holster all ready to draw, eyes squinting straight ahead.

'I'm calling you.'

He knows there should be trail dust blowing in the air between them, a hot sun in a deep blue sky, tumbleweeds being lifted and rolled along the empty main street, the townsfolk hiding indoors waiting to see which one of them's left standing afterwards. He knows he should be the one walking away, that slow walk back to his office with the Winchesters in their rack behind his desk and the bunch of jail keys in the top drawer. That's what always happens. But since that night in the alley everything's slashed red from side to side, and instead of the hot wind blowing in from the desert there's only the stillness of the painted scenery – the streets, the pavements and tenements.

Till a moment ago. Till he looked over and saw the varmint himself stepping out the doorway and into the street – with the same rage and madness that came thundering towards him in the lane that night. And so...

The Sheriff and Susie and Swanny

Action! Like the film had been badly cut and jumped straight from the night scene in the alley to *now*. From the girl's screaming – to *this*.

The Sheriff has had to take a few steps backwards to keep his balance after that store-clerk pushed past him rushing to get clear of the street before the shooting started.

He's called out to that no-good critter in the doorway, giving him one last chance to make his play.

'Step out where I can see you, or step out – shooting!'

Then all at once he feels the trail dust blowing in the air between them. He feels the brightness of the hot sun, the emptiness of the deep blue sky, the tumbleweeds drifting past, the townsfolk watching and waiting indoors. Still steadying himself as best he can, still trying to stay on his feet. 'I'm taking you in, you varmint!'

With her perfect view of the street below Susie has seen everything: the two men talking, the lab guy shoving the mad sheriff to one side and then limping away as fast as he can. The sheriff has staggered back, light as a puff of wind. He nearly falls over but manages to stay on his feet. Keeps stumbling all over the place and shouting, right in the middle of the road. Shouting at the other lab guy, who's now appeared in the doorway. That's when she catches sight of the car coming round the corner.

She knows what's going to happen next, she wants to look away, but can't.

The old man rises weightlessly into the air and hangs there, it seems to her, for several seconds. There's a thump as he lands on the bonnet and begins to slide forward. The car's come to a standstill. The sheriff is lying face down on the road.

Swanny's already well clear of the crazy cowboy when he hears the shouting and yelling behind him get suddenly louder. Big Brother Barry must have found out that he's run off – his cue to keep moving.

That screaming, that terrible screaming – Susie puts her hands to her ears and steps back from the window. *Close the curtains*, she hears herself say, *close the curtains and keep safe*. She continues backing away from the window, every step she takes frightens her more than the last.

The Sheriff knows he's not going to make it, not this time. Already the townsfolk have come rushing out of their houses and are standing around him. He knows it's too late.

He can't seem to speak any more and can taste a warm stickiness that'll soon be trickling from the side of his mouth in a red stream. He's seen men die before. It's his turn now.

The varmint must have hit leather, gone for his gun without even making a fair call. But he'll get what's coming to him, one day – payback for what he did to that girl. Before the credits start to roll someone'll ride into town and fix him, someone'll even the score. That's what always happens. Always.

One more evening with friends and kangaroos

Phil caught sight of several grey-haired twins in the mirror, and double-smiled at them.

'Bastards, and you're drunk the lot of you.'

He splashed some water on his face. No paper towels – so he had to use the hand-dryer, which blasted full-force or else cut out completely if he missed it even by a couple of inches. Off/on/off/on. He gave up. Having checked that the many twins had merged themselves back into one, he started out on the long-haul return to his seat.

Franco's Office Bar – a windowless room of broken-down tables, chairs and drunks, beer alcove in one corner, toilet alcove in the other – was at its best late on. Evenings never started in Franco's but often ended up in the blur of its straightforward aim: to get drunks drunker. It was the place where no one felt out of place, ever. For the last three hours he, Mike and Steve had been sitting round a table steadied by the torn beer mats they'd jammed under one of the legs.

Phil crash-landed himself back in front of his pint, to find Mike still on about holidays.

'What you're saying about last-minute flights is all very well, Steve, but the problem with self-catering…'

Phil's elbow slid off the edge of the table – always a bad sign.

'Haud steady, eh! For Christ's sake!' Steve lifted his pint clear.

Mike started on about ABTA; Steve brought in ATOL and charter regulations.

Then Steve wasn't there any more.

Phil had been to Skye, once. He chose a clear stretch of the table, carefully lowered and positioned his elbow dead-centre for balance, and let the rest of him follow.

'I was in Skye once. I was ten years old, maybe. The mist—'

Mike had just mentioned Palma, but Phil's own momentum in leaning forwards kept the words coming. 'The mist, I'm saying, first thing in the morning – not to mention all fucking day – when it cleared, I'm saying…'

Steve was putting more pints on the table.

'Bumped into a friend of yours back there.'

Several Steves, like a hand of face-cards, were being shuffled just above him. Out of the deal came a three-pint card trick that hovered over the table till Phil worked out which pint was the real one, and grabbed it, managing to speak at the same time:

'Who?'

Mike was saying: 'You needed to get up early if you wanted to use the swimming pool. See, the way they do it in Majorca is—'

'Who? Who?'

'Turned intae a fucking owl now, have you, Phil?'

'I'm asking – who? That you bumped intae?'

'That friend of yours. The waste of space you lumbered us with before. The paper-bag champion, the boxer.'

'Sonny?'

'That's the clown. Didn't speak to him. Didn't even let on I'd seen him, not after last time.'

'Last time?'

'Him and his hard man act – nearly got us thrown out, remember?'

The shelves behind the bar were moving in time to the noise, and so were the walls: everywhere he turned was looking like scraps of somewhere else, and being blown round and round where he sat. If he stood up he'd maybe not stay up. If, that is, he could get himself to stand...

Grabbing good hold of the table edge...

A few seconds to get himself balanced...

Lifting up his eyes...

'Whereabout?' He'd get Sonny a pint and explain he's with friends. No problem. The only way.

Mike was drawing a diagram and explaining something about air beds.

'Whereabout?' Standing upright, nearly. The entire bar surged up to meet him, then ebbed away a layer at a time.

He kept saying the words he wanted till he got them out loud. 'Whereabout's Sonny? Whereabout's Sonny?'

Then Steve on his left: 'Near the phone, I said. Some state you're in.'

Then Mike on his right: 'Your round next, mind. And don't bring that clown back with you.'

Tables, chairs, people, more tables, one of the chairs came away in his hands. With friends, he'd say. No problem. The toilet was empty this time. Near the phone, Steve said. Swaying but keeping it clear of the shoes. Not so pissed. Not so pissed as to get himself pissed on. Near the phone. Hands washed. Drying them now, or trying to – still no paper towels. Fucking hand-dryer, fucking wind-tunnel, more like. What the -? Kangaroo-flavoured condoms? A joke, no? No. Fucking kangaroo-flavoured right enough. Keep one jump ahead, eh!

Near the phone, Steve had said.

Looking left, looking right and looking straight ahead like a good boy. No Sonny. Thank fuck.

No Sonny, no problem.

No problem, except for getting Franco's attention up this end. Taking a good grip of the bar, his foot keeping the rail steady...

Both bar and rail now steadied, *he* was steadied. Waving his tenner like he was flagging down a cab, he shouted:

'Three pints heavy.'

'Phil, any chance you can make that four—?'

Out of nowhere the Wreck of the Year was standing beside him. Bruises instead of eyes, the rest of him scabs and cuts – and not from this year's shave either. Coat turned up at the sleeves.

Time to make an effort, time to show Sonny they might have been in the same class once upon a time, but not any longer. 'Okay, Sonny. Four it is then.'

'Thanks, Phil. How's it going?'

'Keeping a few jumps ahead. Yourself?'

'Still in the game.'

'So I see.'

'Fucking kids tried taking a lend of me. Bunch of Tiny Tots, but I skelped their arses and seen them off goodstyle. Goodstyle. Cheers, Phil! The wee bastards.'

'Cheers. I'm with friends, you understand. Catch you next time.'

When the rounds came to a stop it was him and Sonny standing outside Franco's. Steve and Mike must have headed off somewhere.

'Tell you Sonny: fucking kangaroos in the toilet!'

'Keeping a jump ahead. Aye, you were saying.'

He was leaning against a wall:

'I'm for offski. See you, Sonny.'

'Which way're ye gang?'

'Hame.'

Then he was holding onto a good solid rone-pipe. 'Grand night, eh? Friends and kangaroos.'

'Which way, Phil? Which way?'

Maybe Sonny was only trying to help, but the man's fucking questions just kept on coming.

'Gang hame, I said.'

'Aye, Phil, but which way're ye gang?'

'Gang where?'

'Eh...? Phil, I said where are ye—?'

'Where we gang?'

'Not me, Phil. You. Which way're ye gang?'

'Hame, I keep telling you. See, there's a cab! Grab it!'

'He'll no stop. One look at you's enough. You can let go the rone now, Phil, and haud ontae me. Like that time at the school, mind?'

'Mind what?'

'At the school – when ye were battering Billy Chambers? Nearly killing him ye were, till I hauled ye off. Ye'd really lost the heid. I'd tae drag you halfway round the playground to get ye calmed down. Mind? Nou, get a guid haud.'

Traffic everywhere he turned, and when he turned too soon the streetlights smeared round with him; the pavement and the road kept tripping him into puddles.

'Left here, Phil. Mind the step. Keep going. And—'

The same traffic, the same puddles, the same streetlights. When he closed his eyes he felt sick. When he opened them he felt worse.

He was leaning against a wet wall. No more traffic, no more puddles, no more streetlights, no more stepping up and stepping down. He could stay leaning there just as he was all night, suit him. Resting, happy as Larry.

'All right, Phil?'

'Fine, Sonny, fine.'

'Nearly there. Doon the stairs. Yin at a time, eh!'

Fucking escalator near enough – and straight onto the deck. Time for another rest.

The two of them were standing in the doorway of a large room; the strip-lighting made him close his eyes. But that sweat smell was enough, that familiar squeak from the wooden floor as they walked across it.

'Home Sweet Home, for the time being anyroad. Some bits and pieces in the back as'll dae for blankets, an ye can doss on yin o these. Nae feather bed, but it does the trick.'

One of the rubber exercise mats seemed to have lifted itself off the ground and was letting him down gently. He was still falling though, even as he was laid down he felt himself falling further and further. Sonny had gone. There was a blanket on top of him.

A laser stab of brightness gouged him out of sleep. He turned over, and the room turned over with him. Shadows, half-darkness, bars of harsh sunlight, the smell of rubber just about curdling his stomach; his head was vice-tight and his eyes were being pressed into their sockets. So long as he wasn't sick... .

Where the hell was he? Back at school it smelt like: the school gym to be exact. A gym at any rate – he could make out sets of dumb-bells, some ropes, weights, wall bars and a punchbag hanging in one corner. A few feet across from him was a mound of towels and dressing-gowns with someone lying underneath, sleeping. A right battered-looking object it was, too. Fucking Sonny, no less: the bruiser and bampot he spent most of his life trying to keep clear of. His mouth felt cracked with thirst, his eyes were gummed half open, half shut. Hangover was going to be a real fucker and getting itself up to full strength.

The night before was like a stack of badly taken photographs he was catching sight of as they tumbled down around him: Steve with a fistful of pints, Sonny and his bruises at the bar, a taxi splashing them, Mike's holidays, the kangaroo condom machine, the basement steps. For some reason he'd woken up remembering Billy Chambers, and how he'd bounced the poor fucker's head off the playground that first day at secondary school.

The older boys had been circling around them, picking them off one at a time and giving them a doing. Nothing too rough – but just enough so they'd not forget their first day. He and Billy Chambers had been the last ones left, standing back to back, trying to hold out until the bell. They'd no chance, of course. Not once they were made to fight each other instead, and told they'd be in for a real hammering if they didn't. Every time they stopped, they got kicked and threatened with a worse kicking to come. He was pretending to punch Billy in the eye but holding back, when he suddenly realised what it was all about – and knew exactly what he had to do.

Next thing, he'd got himself on top and was battering Billy Chambers as hard as he could, really laying into the sorry fucker, while the rest of the boys cheered him on. They loved it. He'd felt great – and the harder he hit, the greater he felt. And that's when Sonny appeared out of nowhere, the fucking cavalry that nobody asked for.

No one had needed saved last night either. Him and Mike and Steve – an evening with friends. A few drinks and a few laughs. He'd been feeling good for once, really good. So what the fuck was Sonny's problem?

Ticking the boxes

Do you want to say something – or should I just start? Is that how it works...you sit there and listen, letting me 'free-associate', talking myself into a state of 'self-realisation', resolving my 'inner conflicts' into a happy face? Is that the way? Meanwhile you'll be ticking off the boxes, the psychobabble boxes:

Death of Father (a big box that one, you might say!) – *Tick*.

Childhood Traumas – *Tick-Tick-Tick*.

Emotional Nourishment – or lack of it – During Formative Years (on a scale of 1–10) – *Tick*.

Body Language – *Tick*.

That how it works?

Hmm...Okay, I'll keep on talking – seeing as how I'm paying for it, like some golf bore who thinks buying you a drink allows him to replay his whole game to you, stroke by stroke. Just as the world's divided into takers and givers, so it splits into talkers and listeners. Usually I'm a listener – which suits me fine. Standing at the bar while someone trundles on about the state of the world or their garden, I'm quite happy to nod and grunt 'Oh yes', 'Really?', 'Surely not!' – without listening to a word that's said.

This time, though, I'll do the talking if that's what's wanted – but what do you want me to talk about? I've not really got much to say. This and that, I suppose. Things. Nothing special. Like I said, I'm not really a talker. Same at work. When McDougall, our Area Manager, starts on with his thoughts about some Head Office directive or strategy initiative, I switch off and put myself into nod-and-grunt mode. Result – he's happy, and I...Well, I'm being paid for getting through the day whatever happens. So we're both happy, I suppose.

Am I happy? Sure. I've ticked all the boxes on that one.

Nice wife – *Tick*.

Nice Kids – *Tick-Tick*.

House with garage – *Tick and a half*!

Company Car, Company Pension – *Tick-Tick*.

Private Health Scheme – *Tick*.

Two Foreign Holidays per Year – *Tick-Tick*.

Yes, even after all that's happened I can still tick the right boxes. The Happy Boxes! Even when my father...

No, that's ancient history. Been there, done that – *tick-tick*. Three months ago it was, and him up a ladder like I'd told him not to. I said I'd call round early evening to change the bulb for him. But no, not him, not Mr Self-Made Man. He couldn't wait. A summer's day with the full sun beaming megawatts into his kitchen and he just had to get up that ladder and change the bulb himself. He knew I was coming round later, coming round specially to put that bulb in for him. He *knew* that. And I was near enough on time. Five, ten minutes late at most. I can be relied on – he *knew* that.

It was him all over, of course. The self-made man. Started his own business from scratch. Paterson's Packaging – 'You make it, we'll crate it.' Every single night it seemed like, he'd relive his struggle from rags-to-riches round the family dinner table, action-replaying his successes deal by deal while my mum, my sister Pam and me sat there, nodding and grunting out our 'Reallys' and 'My goodnesses' between mouthfuls.

Weekends were even worse. I remember one time when we went fishing…

Hold it. That's *really* ancient history – a lifetime ago it was. Listen, I've come to see you because I'm not sleeping so well and Rosie, my wife, thought you'd be able to help. So here I am. I go to bed exhausted, my head hits the pillow – and at once I'm more wide awake than I've been all day. I lie there staring up at the ceiling – my body like lead, my mind in overdrive. I've tried everything – sleeping tablets, milky drinks, herbal remedies, relaxation tapes, brandy. Useless. I'm not worrying or anything – just can't sleep. I get one to two hours at most, and come morning I'm more worn out than ever. As for a few dreams to help 'unlock the subconscious' – well, I never sleep long enough to dream anything.

When I do manage to nod off it's just a blank, like getting shut up in an empty box. He's in his box, you might say, and I'm in mine.

That's what he really wanted, you understand. Both of us in boxes – in Paterson's Packaging. 'Paterson & Son' he was hoping to call it. Plan was – *his* plan, of course, like always – that I'd join the firm when I left school. Start at the bottom and work myself up into management, in a fast-track imitation of his own success-story. Christ, what a nightmare that would have been! Bad enough having him bossing me around at home evenings and weekends without it being all day, every day, as well.

So I said no. He insisted. I still said no. Meanwhile I'm frantically looking round for another job, anything. And I struck lucky – the day after I left school I got myself started as a clerk in a factory making ball-bearings. Our motto was: 'Whatever the job, Baxter's have the balls for it!' Make what you will of that, Mr Freud! And now, thanks to nodding and grunting at the right time to the right people, I run a whole department.

Paterson's Packaging went bust nearly a year back, and my father with it. I felt sorry for him. Naturally. Tried to help him, but he wouldn't take any help, from me least of all. Fact is, he was too stuck in his ways – all that self-made stuff belongs to last century. Business practice has moved on, it's all about teamwork now. With him it was just boxes and more boxes till the bottom fell out!

But I felt really sorry for him. I really did. Then, six months later, when I called round to change that bulb for him...I find him...lying there on the floor. Must have lost his balance and tumbled from the ladder. He looked smaller, like an old-man doll with the stuffing...

No, I *don't* dream about him. I don't dream, I told you. Are you not listening?

I don't dream because I don't sleep. That's why I'm here, remember?

Sorry, I didn't mean to start on about my father; I had enough of him while he was alive...

Sorry again, I didn't mean it like it sounded. Fits me right into the Freudian box, that does! Here's how that box probably goes:

Subconsciously I knew he'd not wait for me to call round and would try to climb up the ladder by himself.

Which is why I told him I wouldn't go round until a bit later... and got there even later than I'd said.

Which means I killed him, or my subconscious did! Tick the psychobabble box!

Which is why I feel guilty.

My guilt is stopping me from sleeping. Subconsciously, of course.

Is that how it goes, doctor?

Except that it's simply not true.

The problem is that, these days, you can't open a magazine or watch TV without catching someone psychobabbling about something. Thanks to all these reality shows, to Jerry Springer and 'Know Yourself' articles, we all 'understand' our behaviour. We're learning to tick the psychobabble boxes for ourselves. At this rate, how long before you yourself are made redundant, with a crate-load of boxes all your very own to deal with? 'Lack of Self-Esteem', 'Identity Crisis', 'Negative-Reinforcement', you name it. Every box'll be empty, just like your days and nights. Like my father, you'll have nothing to live for. And that's when you'll get to know real fear, real terror – for that's the emptiest box of all, the empty box that's waiting just for you. By then *you* won't be able to sleep either – for fear you don't wake, ever!

Not me though. I'm fine. I can't sleep…simply because I can't sleep, end of story. Maybe I work too hard, who knows? Any suggestions? Any good advice? That's why I'm here, after all.

Apart from the sleeping – the not-sleeping, I mean – I'm a happy man, as you can see. I've worked hard to get where I am. Now that I'm head of the department I can put my feet up and let my staff do all the work. I deserve it. No? If I want, I can retire in ten years on a good pension. The kids'll be paying their way by then, leaving me to play golf, do a bit of DIY, help Rosie to look after her garden…with jaunts abroad whenever the mood takes us. Perfect, eh! What more could a man want? I might even take up fishing again – not very PC, I know, but…

Yes, I used to go fishing with him, believe it or not. Well, one time at any rate…But that's ancient history, like I said. Hardly even remember it.

No, it's not that I don't *want* to remember it. I'm not 'in denial'. It was nothing, just a stupid, stupid…Christ, it was nothing.

Correction – it was him all over.

Yes, I am angry. Who wouldn't be?

You really want to hear it?

Okay, I'll tell you. But it was nothing special. Nothing 'traumatic'. Just *stupid*.

Right? Sitting comfortably? Then I'll begin.

It was the weekend. A Saturday. I was about nine or ten years old. Let's all go fishing, he said. Even though we'd never gone fishing before, I knew exactly what would happen: Mum would make sandwiches and a flask of tea, then she and my sister would sit on the bank while I faffed around not knowing what I was doing while he did the real fishing like the big hero he was. Which is exactly what happened. He kitted up his second-best rod (Freudian, or what?) for me, put a worm on the hook for me, cast it into the river for me, then stuck the rod in my hands telling me to keep my eyes on the float. Okay so far?

So I watch this yellow cork thing bobbing on the water while he gets his best rod prepared.

It is a beautiful summer's day with reflections of the clear blue sky and occasional flecks of white clouds drifting on the water. The air is still and warm, not a breath of wind. I feel really happy standing there on the bank, holding my fishing rod, watching the float…and hoping with all my heart I'll catch something. That'd show him! I'd be so proud, and everyone – my mum, my sister and even Mr Hero Fisherman himself – would be amazed. 'Please, fish,' I whisper. 'Please swim near and…'

Then it happens. One moment my float's bobbing in the water, and the next it's vanished. There's a fierce tug on the line. My rod's suddenly bent like a bow, the reel's screeching, the line unwinding too fast for me to stop it. I hold on for all I'm worth, shouting, 'A fish! A fish! I've got a fish!'

I didn't know what to do *except* hold on. He could have told me, of course, talked me through it – it wasn't a big fish, I could easily have managed. He could have stood behind me, reaching his arms round me even, and placed his hands on mine to guide me.

But he didn't. Not him.

'Give it here,' he says, snatching the rod out of my hands.

For the next five minutes I had to look on while he played the fish – my fish! – and landed it, all the while giving me a running commentary on his technique. So that I could learn the right way to do things, he told me. As if I cared. Like I said, it was nothing.

When my mum cooked it for tea that evening, I refused to eat any. When I was made to – I sicked it all up and was sent to bed. I remember lying in the darkness for hours, hating him.

But, like I say, that was years ago. Ancient history. Tick the Childhood Trauma box, and let's move on.

All I want is a good night's sleep. You listening? All I want's to close my eyes and rest. He's resting now – so why can't I? Sometimes when I'm lying there tense and stiff – like rigor mortis almost! – my wife holds me and soothes me, and I can feel her touch, her gentleness, starting to melt away all the sadness inside me...

And I get so scared...scared that *everything* will melt away till there's nothing left of me. Nothing.

I didn't want him dead. I didn't. You believe me, don't you?

Don't you?

Temptations from an ancient world

I. Eurydice considers the colours of hell

Closing every door and locking it. Down the green linoleum passage:

The kitchen door – *click*. 'Locked.'

The living-room door – *click*. 'Locked.'

The bathroom door – *click*. 'Locked.'

Your bedroom – *click*. 'Locked.'

Your mother's room – *click*. 'Locked.'

Into the old shoes for the garbage and dogshit of the world outside.

Into the old clothes for the noise you don't want brought back home.

Closing the front door. A pause of satisfaction – everything in the house is now fixed in position, locked and safe until your return. Even if the angriest god picked the house up now and shook it, there would be no unfastened doors to swing open, no windows to be rattled loose and break.

Down the cement path, your right hand on the wrought-iron gate, lifting the stiff catch...

Wait. Pause. There might be a patch of sun in the living-room, drawing layer upon layer of colour from your mother's carpet – that heavy-piled maroon-black inheritance must be protected against children, men, dogs, visitors and daylight. Are the blinds fully down? Or did you raise them in a moment of forgetfulness? Should you go back and make sure?

No. You're not one of that fussy spinsterhood who switch off their gas at the cooker, at the wall, then at the mains – doing everything ten times to be sure it's been done once. When you do something, there's always a part of you looking on to check, to keep things right. You can trust yourself – and how many can say that!

Home again. To make certain the kitchen knives have not blunted in your absence you lay them out on the table, trying each in turn.

On with the radio: background noise to serve as a whetstone for your resolve. Adverts, international news, local news, an interview with a politician. How can you reconcile the dirt and grime, the down-and-outs, the diesel and litter of the street you live in, with such ingratiating nonsense? Not that you need to – you have the power to turn these voices off and on at will, so let them speak. They're a strop to each blade's sharpness, nothing more.

Finally, testing the separation of light into its perfect spectrum as you angle the knife-edge to an almost perfect balance of silvered steel and total concentration. Examine the reflections: the kitchen cupboard behind you, then your face, then the red, yellow and green metallic flames sliding to invisibility at the tip.

A glimpse into life's mysteries, you might joke to yourself. You have to joke sometimes. But there's no real mystery, is there? Not to life anyway. Watching your mother die in her room: legs, liver, bowels, kidneys and all the other parts packing up one at a time until nothing worked. No mystery, no pot of gold at the end of the rainbow.

More volume on the radio. You're not going deaf – only, you need a moment's distraction now and again. We all do. Keep the knives sharp and ready – that's all that matters.

Waiting, waiting…It's when you feel yourself most alone that he'll appear. He can charm his way through locked doors, he can even enter your dreams to seek you out. He'll flatter you; he'll be a mouthful of promises and reassurances. He'll look concerned and strong. He'll understand you and offer you everything: the future and hope.

Until then, you need not be afraid: remember who you are and that you are safe. Even if this is Hell, you have seen its burning colours and made them your own. Cherish what they have branded onto your heart.

2. Orpheus seeking refuge

You know what is going to happen: this same rush of lust always comes as you enter her part of town. In less than ten minutes she'll open her door, smile and take you into the sitting-room. There will be a polished wooden table by her window, set with an opened bottle, glasses, small dishes of nuts, olives and gherkins; lace curtains hold back the light. As the traffic's busy, you're having to wait at the corner of Nicolson Square. Soon you'll be sitting beside her: some small talk, light-hearted/serious as the mood suggests, keeping things friendly and pleasant, giving her your full attention, watching her closely, waiting for the right moment.

The nearer you come to her house the more the street begins to seem it isn't really there. When the lights change you cross to the florist's: a few words with the shopkeeper, a joke with him even, but all the time everything's growing more unreal around you, more like a copy of Nicolson Square than the place itself. If you look too closely you might see the flaws.

That's *you* in the nearest shop window: a man in his forties, slightly greying, slightly stooped, but with plenty of life in the old dog yet. No? Another glance to make sure, tugging up the corners of your mouth into a smile, narrowing your eyes to show depth of feeling. Convincing, aren't you? Or more like a teenager inspecting his latest hairstyle, and asking, 'Is this me?'

While you're standing there you sense a draught blowing into your face as though coming from beneath, up through a gap between the paving stones, and carrying with it the sweet dampness of decay. You'd better concentrate for a moment, picture to yourself the dress you asked her to wear, the sexy one with buttons up the front. Yes, that dress, and the faded print of clowns with their balloons and coloured streamers above her living-room fire, the handstitched rug, the glass-fronted bookcase, the black leather sofa. You believe that such accumulated detail is reassuring; maybe it is, who knows?

It was crossing the road that reminded you: for a split-second you glimpsed water swirling and hissing over rocks some twelve feet below, and the wooden footbridge you're being forced to crawl across, so rotted that many of the planks are missing altogether. There's no handrail, the whole length sways, creaks and swings as you inch forward on your hands and knees. Once again you hear the clamour and jeering of the boys who've already made it over; behind you, the silence of those still waiting their turn. You've stopped halfway across: no way forward, no way back, and only your fear, it seems, to cling to.

A long time ago, and not worth remembering. Surely what really matters is the evening ahead. First thing when you arrive you'll greet her and give her the flowers. She'll offer you a drink. You'll sit together on the sofa, she'll be wearing the short, sexy dress. You'll ask her how she is, what she's been doing; you'll listen, seem interested. You know what's going to happen, and so does she.

Eventually, of course, you did reach the other side. Your little brother was to come after. You watched him pick his way carefully, testing where to put his weight. Within a few yards of you he looked up and grinned – the next second, his foot had gone through one of the rotted planks. He was shouting for help, screaming and screaming. The bridge thrummed with his frantic struggling to get hold of something solid while more and more of the rotten woodwork gave way. Before you knew what you were doing you'd scrambled back to help him.

Was it because of your extra weight? His panic? With a dry crack the section of the wood he was gripping split in two, upended and fell into the river. You'd almost got your hand to him...

Even as you peered over the edge of the hole he'd tumbled through, your first thought was: if you hadn't gone back to save him, maybe he would have crossed safely. Some of the boys burst into tears, some turned and ran.

Such a long time ago. Forget it. You should hurry or you will be late. You'll ring the bell, greet her, give her the flowers, then it's through to her sitting-room. A few minutes' chat, a kiss; the buttons on the front of her dress, the cushions on the floor. But gradually these things too will seem more and more like a copy – of this visit, of the one before and the one before that. Towards the end you'll need to force yourself to listen to her and it'll be an effort to continue holding her in your arms. Not because you don't care enough, but because nothing, not even love itself, can raise the dead.

The water was deep enough for his body to be completely covered. His blue T-shirt, swollen by the current, billowed up from his chest, his hair was lifted like pale weed, his left leg looked stuck on backwards, the bone of his right jutted out through his jeans; around him the river bubbled bright red. Downstream, after the narrow rush under the bridge, there was a stretch of calm: some geese, startled by the sudden shouting, were settling back on the still surface, a few brown and white cattle stood on the bank staring, it seemed, down at their reflections. The sky was divided unevenly by a white trail of jet exhaust.

No matter how many times you tell yourself it wasn't your fault, you'll never believe it. If it happened again, you would do exactly the same, wouldn't you? Without thinking you'd rush back to help, try to save him; the rotted planks would give way and he would fall – again and again and again…A death and a life: and you passing back and forth between them as if it's all you can ever know.

So, here's her front door. Now ring the bell. Greet her: be kind to her and let her be kind to you. Find refuge in each other's arms for as long as you can bear.

By the time you leave, everything around you will be solid and real once more. A final wave, remember, and a smile before going down the path back to the street. The moment when you turn away is the moment when she'll know for certain who you are. Don't worry though, she always forgets until the next time. And so do you.

3. Jason and the Golden Fleece

Some of you are just looking for a bit of fun, I don't mind that. There's not a lot of it about and I'm no killjoy. If it's a dance you're after I could manage something – a sailor's hornpipe, probably. But why pester an old guy sitting on his bench? Look at me! Look at my hands and face and what's left of the hair, the clothes and the old shoes…Not a pretty sight, as the man said. And my eyes, pools of uncertainty so I've been told. Beats me what holds it all together. Each time I wake up I say to myself: 'Still here, eh!'

I'm a survivor, let's leave it at that. Ask any of them around here. 'Jason?' they'll say, 'He's doing all right. A survivor.'

Think I'm kidding? One look inside my poly-bag here, and you'd be surprised. Delighted even. Yes, as the man said, life's a thing of mystery.

I've no complaints.

Know my secret? It's simple. Too simple for most folk, but I'll tell you: I believe in facts. Simple as that. To me, one fact's worth more than a thousand hopes and promises. All that sort of stuff's for the birds. And I'll tell you what kind. Vultures. The vultures that tear out your living heart.

My father, for example, had no chance, even though he was a king. The vultures smelt him out, swooped down – and gorged themselves.

Look, suppose it was you sitting at home in your palace, waiting for the return of your dearly beloved son Jason. You're ageing and hope's running out more with every year. The place is going to rack and ruin – you don't give a toss any more. The Golden Fleece? All you want is your boy Jason back home safe. The gold and silver, the splashing fountains, the marble halls and slave girls – who needs them?

Gradually, of course, word gets round: 'There's an old fool with plenty of the ready to shell out for news of his darling son.' Before you know it, you're overrun with honest merchants and travellers, each with a story to tell. You encourage them, you want to hear what they've got to say – who wouldn't?

Your own people, the priests, courtiers and so forth, begin to feel a little threatened. 'Wait a minute, Your Highness,' they insist. 'This is the phonus-balonus you're getting.'

And so, who needs faithful servants? Let's have the phonus-balonus – at least it gets you through the day. That's all that matters now: out of bed, out of the palace, through the pleasure-gardens and straight to the cliff tops to see if there's a ship, your son's ship.

The baloney merchants, of course, can't be too helpful. 'Maybe today,' they tell you. And if you're looking particularly down, a bit of extra baloney about how they'd heard that just along the coast a ship had been...

And look at you go! Hopping along the cliff edge! 'But it's not reached here yet!' they shout. You wait, and so another day passes.

Naturally you get suspicious, especially at mealtimes. You can't help but notice the way they guzzle at the roast meats, their chins running with gravy and wine, and keep touching up the maids. You can't always hear what they're saying, or what they're laughing at. Later, as you're leaving to go to bed, up they come, one at a time, to show how much they care, a hand on the shoulder perhaps, for a quiet, serious word: 'Maybe tomorrow, let us hope and pray.' Then a look, a sincere look that gets you right between the eyes.

In bed you lie watching the stars. You like to think that perhaps, just then, your son Jason, too, is gazing up at the same night sky to chart his way home. And for those few moments you don't hear the singing and laughter coming up from the main hall.

Of course you're suspicious but, apart from a few distant stars that couldn't care less, what else is there? On bad nights, when you can't sleep for the worrying and for the partying downstairs, you imagine the phonus-balonus crowd have already killed your son. After all, with him out the road, they'd be safely on the gravy-train right to the end of the line. A terrible thought, and nothing to be done about it. You keep it for the worst moments.

Doubtless, though, they're watching from the cliff tops even more anxiously than you are. They'll want to get to Jason first. To explain, to soften him up. They're not really evil men – they're after an easy life, that's all, a good berth. Chances are when your son does arrive they'll just pack up and move on. But sometimes, on very bad nights, you remember a look in their eyes and you're not so sure.

So, like it or not, every night's party night. The rot's getting to you, you're after the best of both worlds: just enough anxiety to keep you on your toes while knowing there's reassurance on tap, as much as you want and whenever you want it.

Then one night something new occurs to you: if your son's ship has its golden sail hoisted to announce his safe return, perhaps it won't mean such good news after all – but, rather, a knife in the back. First you, then him.

And so, first thing next morning, it's down to the cliffs with the baloney-boys. Don't stand too close, you're thinking – and yet you need to hear your daily dose of hope. One moment you're wanting the golden sail to appear and the next you're not.

The big day's bound to dawn sooner or later. Will it feel any different? The sun will rise, the morning chill lift, the sky will be cloudless, the sea an Adriatic blue, heat-shimmer, the works – and in the distance, a ship. The baloney-merchants will be pressing even closer, crying out:

'A sail! A sail!'

But what colour of sail? And who can tell at that distance? They're hard at it, cheering themselves hoarse:

'Welcome home, Jason!' They turn to you with smiles and bright eyes and, you're quite sure, turn away in fury. What colour? The gold of a safe return, or black? The Band of Hope begins closing in.

Picture the scene that morning: there's hardly a breath of wind, the ship's tacking from side to side towards the shore, catching the sun and then being caught in its shadow. One moment the centre sail's golden, the next – black as night. Here's me, Jason. Safe and sound, and surviving so far. I'm returning with the Golden Fleece after years at sea. Maybe it's been ten years, maybe ten thousand. It's all ancient history, you might say.

Well, don't. On my way back I've had plenty of time to think things through. I warn you, I've not come all this way for nothing, to be got drunk at some welcome-home party, then quietly bumped off by freeloaders. Afterwards they'd tell you I was a fraud; or else pretend the whole thing was a dream and that there'd been no ship, no sail, no beloved son.

So, if I'm to survive on that big day, I've no choice in the sail. As the man said, Any colour you want, so long as it's black. When you see it, there's a chance you might throw yourself off the cliffs with grief, or your heart might give way. I'm sorry, but there's nothing I can do about that. I'm a survivor, remember.

Well, time's getting on. What's your pleasure? A dance? I said I could give you a hornpipe. Or a song, 'Sixteen Men on a Dead Man's Chest'? For fifty pence you can have a look at the Golden Fleece here in my poly-bag.

Taking care of Mother

Anna has always known the meaning of *good*: if a black was disrespectful, her father would beat him with one of his handmade whips while everyone in the small leatherwork factory and household, including her, was assembled to look on. One particularly hot afternoon her father had been in the middle of carrying out a punishment for lateness when, with his arm raised to full stretch, he'd screamed, dropped his whip and fallen face down in the dirt. By the end of the following day he had been laid to rest, and by the end of the following week the factory was closed. Even though she'd recently turned forty, Anna insisted she remain to run the small health clinic she had set up, and more than fifteen years were to pass before she followed her mother back to Scotland. By then, it was clear that the old woman needed looking after.

Taking care of Mother was pleasant enough at first. The problems came whenever people in the village questioned Anna about conditions in the new South Africa – what she still prefers to call the *race situation*. At first she told them about the small clinic where she'd tried to teach hygiene and contraception, had bandaged sores and given injections – but she soon learnt to save her breath. How could any of these do-gooders understand what living among blacks was really like? Know-alls like them wanted to feel superior, that was all, and demonstrate a worldly tolerance for which there was no scope in their wet grey little Scottish village.

She'd arrived in mid-November, when the days are dark and the nights long. After a grim few weeks, when it became clear that everyone in the village knew everyone else and she still knew no one, she decided to go to the Christmas Sale of Work. The minister greeted her and introduced her to a Mrs Collingwood with the words: 'You two ladies should get to know each other – you have a great deal in common.'

Anna feels nervous as she turns off the road and walks through the gateless entrance: a pair of ten-foot high pillars marks the only gap in the massive stone wall around the grounds. Purple and red rhododendron bushes line the gravel path; between the bare branches of oak and beech she can see tall chimneys set in a sea of slates. She passes an archway leading to a courtyard of moss-covered cobbles, empty stables and roofless outbuildings; the tennis court has a permanently off-season feel with its rotted posts, weeds and no net. Mrs Collingwood had told her they'd lived in Zimbabwe before selling up their farm a few years back. They'd got out only just in time, she said. As Anna walks up the drive to the large sandstone house, she reminds herself that here, at least, there should be no awkward questions.

The moment she's shown into the bay-windowed sitting-room she knows she's done right in accepting the older woman's invitation. The set of carved masks that hangs along one wall and the ebony figurines clustered here and there on the bookshelves and mantelpiece all seem to be greeting her warmly; and Mrs Collingwood herself is clearly pleased to see her again:

'I'm so very glad you could come – we're sure to have so much to chat about together. You were in South Africa, you said?'

As she tells her mother later, the afternoon simply flew past. They talked about the wonderful African countryside, the heat, the smells, the animals, the blacks, her clinic, her father's factory, the Collingwoods' farm and the changes under the likes of Mandela and Mugabe. They had tea, some cakes. Anna brought out a few photographs, and so did Mrs Collingwood. It was well after five when the two of them parted.

She repeats Mrs Collingwood's words of goodbye: 'You must come again soon, Anna. It's so nice to chat with someone who really *understands* what one is talking about.'

After dinner, Anna helps her mother upstairs to the bathroom. She sees to her needs, washes her, dries her, then puts her to bed. She switches off the electric blanket and makes sure the red emergency call-button is within reach. Anna is bending over her to say the customary 'Sleep well, Mother' and kiss her goodnight, when the old woman grabs her and hisses:

'Your father is a good man.' The unblinking eyes stare into hers: '*Good* – do you understand?'

'Good? Of course.'

'You must never forget that.'

'I won't, Mother.'

'So we must be sure to tell him.'

'In our prayers?'

'You can tell him to his face, can't you?'

'To his face?…Mother?'

With a sigh the old woman lies back down on the bed. 'When he comes in from the workshop – be sure to go to him and tell him. Don't wait. There's a good girl.'

Next morning, as usual, they have breakfast together in the glassed-over rear porch her mother calls the *conservatory*. Layer upon layer of black cloud seem only just inches above them, heavy rain is drumming loudly onto the panes, and through the streaming glass the garden has a sodden underwater look. Against this shifting backdrop her mother's movements – the awkward lifting and replacing of her cup, the clumsy bites at her piece of toast – are turned into puppet-like jerks of spoiled coordination, as if the rainwater, or some crueller element, has already got into the works.

From time to time Anna leans over to wipe dribbles from the slackened mouth. All at once the old woman jerks her head free.

'My daughter's in Africa, you know.'

'Yes, Mother, I was there for nearly—'

'My daughter is in Africa, in South Africa to be precise.'

Anna pretends she hasn't heard. 'Would you like me to turn up the fire a little?'

There's no response.

Breakfast over, the old woman sits back, stretches out her hands and starts picking at the loose skin.

'Anna takes care of the natives, you know. She takes good care of them. She's a saint. I keep all her letters. I must show them to you some time.' Then a glance and a smile, 'Yes, you're right, it *is* rather cold. Another bar would be a kindness.'

After crouching down to re-set the switch, Anna gets to her feet and, without meaning to, finds herself staring down at her mother's trembling hands, at the criss-cross of discoloured markings and veins. They're like a nest she'd been shown once out in the bush: coil upon seething coil of black and vermilion snakes.

It rains most of the weekend. Sunday morning begins with a few patches of blue sky, a watery blue that soon darkens to daylong twilight. The two women watch TV, eat their meals, and about eight o'clock Anna helps her mother upstairs.

She's getting her settled when the old woman sits up, her face radiant as she points to the foot of the bed:

'Look! Look! Isn't it beautiful!'

Anna looks, but can see nothing.

'So beautiful! So beautiful!' Her mother is almost ecstatic, her hands straining forwards: 'The sun! The sun! Let me touch. Please, please let me touch!'

'You should lie down, Mother. It's time to sleep. Come on.' Anna does her best to ease her back down: 'Come on, Mother. We'll get you comfortable.'

'But I want to touch the sun. It's there. Let me touch it. Please, please.' She begins to sob. A moment later she seems to have lost interest and slumps back against the pillows.

Anna straightens the covers. 'Feeling better now, Mother? I'll leave the night-light on, and the bell's there if you need me. Sleep well.'

The old woman gazes up at her. 'My usual nanny's black, who are you?'

'But, Mother…'

'*You*'re not my mother. I know you're not.' Then, like a sullen child, she turns her face to the wall and pretends to go to sleep.

Anna's·second visit to her new friend starts with a cup of tea and more talk about Africa. Then Colly – as Mrs Collingwood now insists she call her – pours them out some sherry. Very soon Anna begins to feel light-headed. To her surprise she's found herself talking about her mother.

'Must be very hard,' Colly's saying. 'I doubt if I could cope… Take the patience of a saint, I'd imagine.'

Another sip of sherry, and Anna feels her head swim pleasantly. 'I do what I can, that's all.'

'Always have, it seems. Looking after the people at your clinic, and now taking care of your mother. What about you?'

'Me?' She laughs, she's deliciously dizzy now. 'What about me?'

'Well, if you don't mind my asking, who's ever looked after *you*?'

The pleasant dizziness just seems to be going on and on.

'My mother's always done what she thought right.'

Not quite what she meant to say, but it doesn't seem to matter. Anna sinks back into the couch, into the relaxing smell of the leather. So familiar, like one of those hot days when she'd sit in the veranda shade, the air sweetly acrid with the smell of the freshly tanned skins stacked in bundles waiting for the lorry to take them to the rail depot for Jo'burg. Letting her eyes close, she can easily imagine herself still under the clear blue skies of Africa.

When it's time to leave, her coat just will not go on. She feels a proper fool standing there in the hall, her arm jammed halfway down one sleeve while she struggles with the other. Colly has started to laugh.

'Anna, I'm sorry but – that's actually *my* coat you're trying on.'

'Oh! Excuse me! Please excuse me!'

'An easy mistake – nearly the same colour.'

How could she have got them mixed up? Colly's being kind, of course.

'Allow me, madam,' the older woman holds her coat for her, pretending to be an attendant.

'Thank you.' Anna trembles as she puts first one arm into the sleeve, then the other. A perfect fit.

'You must be sure to come again, madam. You look splendid now.'

'Thank you, I'm sorry to have made such a terrible mistake. So *embarrassing*.' She is aware of her hostess behind her, straightening the lie of the collar on her shoulders.

'I'd have got the best of the bargain! Anyway, Anna, that's what friends are for – when I was a girl we were always swapping clothes for those nights out that were going to change our lives!'

'Yes, I suppose…'

'Don't think about it.' Colly opens the front door and adds, in a more serious tone of voice, 'I do hope we become friends.'

'Yes, friends…' Anna hesitates, not sure exactly what she wants to say. 'That would be…good.' She turns to glance outside. 'At least it's not raining any more.'

Having taken her leave she hurries off down the drive. Mother will be needing looked after.

During their evening meal, the old woman keeps talking on and on about Anna, her wonderful daughter, who runs the health clinic. Anna is so kind, Anna is so good.

'Gets paid a pittance, of course. There's no money, equipment's always breaking down, the natives steal – but Anna just works all the harder. She's a good person. Could have been married a dozen times over, of course, but has chosen a life of selfless dedication. Naturally, grandchildren would have been nice, but still…'

'Mother, please. Don't you know me?'

'Her father can tell you all about her, if you didn't mind waiting a moment. He'll be back shortly, he's out in the yard teaching some blacks a lesson in respect. Can't you hear?'

'Hear what, Mother?'

The old woman edges a little forward in her chair: there is a faint knowing smile, then she flinches. '*That*…and *that*. It's his duty, his responsibility…'

Two hours later as Anna helps her mother upstairs the old woman suddenly pushes her away, shouting,

'Who are *you*? Who are you? Where's Anna, where's my daughter Anna? Leave me alone.' Pausing halfway up the stairs to gaze blankly about her, she calls out, 'Anna! Anna!'

They carry on, step after step. Then, almost at the top, her mother pushes her away again. This time with such force that Anna stumbles, both hands grabbing for the banister rail.

Having steadied herself she turns in time to see her mother

staggering backwards, struggling to regain her balance...and failing. And screaming.

As if everything is happening in slow-motion, she watches the old woman claw at the empty air, then go tumbling down the entire flight of stairs – hitting her head against the banister, against the wall.

Seconds later her mother is lying at the bottom, a smashed huddle. She's moaning. But still alive.

Anna's brought herself some breakfast through on a tray to the conservatory. It's very early, but she knows she can't afford to linger, there's a great deal to be done – the undertaker to deal with, and the minister. There are phone calls to make, letters to write, her mother's papers to sort through. As she sips her first cup she senses the weight of guilt threatening to descend on her once more and crush her.

For the third time that morning she tells herself that facts must be faced: she *panicked*. What other explanation can there be?

Doctor Ross had been furious with her last night. While grabbing his bag he'd yelled at her: Why in God's name had she come all the way over to his surgery? Why hadn't she phoned? Delay like this could mean the difference between life and death. That was when she'd started to cry. It had all happened so quickly, she said. She'd been so confused. The phone at the clinic never worked, you never even thought of using it. As he'd hustled her out to his car she kept repeating, 'The phone never worked. It never worked. I'm sorry. I'm so very sorry.'

Sitting alone in the chilly conservatory, her face uplifted as if she's pleading to the darkness above, Anna's on the verge of tears again.

'I just panicked, that's all. I tried to do what was right. I am a good person. I really am. I never even thought of using the phone…' She says the words aloud, shaking her head for emphasis. 'It's true. It's *true*.'

Just then she catches sight of her reflection in the glass. For several seconds she stares at the neatly brushed hair, the saddened eyes, the tremble in the corner of the mouth – as if she can no longer recognise herself.

The visitor

Hearing there was going to be a special Lucky Dip at Sam's party, Terence punched his fist in the air for joy, 'YES!' then started running up and down the school steps as fast as he could. He ran faster and faster. Not because of the Lucky Dip or the party. Not for anything at all, only a sudden need to punch the sky and to keep running until he crashed over. With the afternoon heat pressing down on him, it felt like he was pounding the sun itself, and couldn't stop...

By the time he was back in class, Terence had calmed down. He sat next to the open window and every so often glanced in the teacher's direction: McBain was telling them the Earth was a greeny-blue dot that hurtled through empty space at hundreds of miles per hour; it turned too steadily for anyone to notice – but they would if it stopped, like when someone slammed on the brakes in a car. UFOs and aliens, he added, were nothing but things on TV. McBain's voice had hit drone-level. The party was going to be in less than three hours. It was always good fun visiting someone else's house: everyone was pleased to see you, and you were pleased to see them. Sam had told him there was going to be a big model ship with red funnels, gangways with tiny stairs between the decks, portholes for the cabins. Best of all, the hold was a Lucky Dip crammed with presents for whoever was invited. Terence had grinned; he and his dad didn't bother much about presents any more.

Hurtling through space or not, there was no sign that the classroom or the village, never mind the whole of planet Earth, was trying very hard to reach four o'clock. Every minute was taking ages. Inside there was the drone of McBain's voice; and outside, the same single-track road as always, the same fields, the same dykes, hedges, trees, the same river, the same everything. He'd told his dad a week ago about Sam's party, told him every day since, and told him again before leaving for school this morning. 'Aye, right,' was all the reply he'd got. His dad had never said, 'You're not going,' or 'Party? I'll party you,' which he might well have done. Just, 'Aye, right.' So his dad knew.

To be on the safe side, though, he'd make sure he was in and out the house before his dad had time to realise he'd even been home. Then he'd vanish into hyperspace – become nothing more than a blur of party-best trainers, jeans and Harry Potter T-shirt going up Mosslands Brae.

They were set to do paired reading and it was Terence's week with the Gom. Time had been crawling along before, but right next to the Gom it came to a complete standstill. It was well-known the Gom could hardly do anything for himself, the rumour was that his mother took her pot scourer to his Gom-face once a week. The Gom tried harder than anyone else in class and, wherever they touched, his hands left sweat marks of effort behind. When it was his own turn to read, Terence planned to keep well clear of Gom-prints, even if the book did have a plastic cover.

He watched the Gom-gaze jerk itself across the page one word at a time:

'The-boy, The-boy-is, The-boy-is-H—, The-boy-is-H—'

At this rate, even three o'clock was never going to come. All around them the rest of the class were seated in pairs facing each other. There was a steady murmur of reading-aloud. From time to time he could hear McBain's voice as the teacher went about the room, correcting mistakes. Terence could see the Gom's eyes boring into the page so hard that if the sticky hands let go, the book would probably stay pinned where it was, in mid-air.

'The-boy-is-H-H—'

'Try it a letter at a time,' Terence whispered.

The Gom took a big swallow of air, then continued, 'The-boy-is H-O-P-I-N-G – hopping-the D-O-G, the dog.' For the first time since he'd started to read, the Gom looked up. 'Hopping the dog?' He looked utterly lost.

Terence was about to laugh out loud when he saw a large tear roll down the Gom's cheek. 'That's right,' he said quickly. 'The boy's hopping the dog. Making it dance, it means maybe. I'll do the next bit.'

He took the book from the Gom, being careful where he put his fingers, and held it right to his face so as not to see the tears the Gom hadn't even sense enough to wipe away.

'The boy is hopping the dog – training it, Gom, teaching it to do tricks, so's it—' he carried on reading: 'will-catch-rabbits-when-they-go-out-later.' He could hear the Gom sniffling and swallowing, but kept on reading to hurry things along and stop the other boy's misery from getting too close. When he was sure that the Gom was back to normal – Gom-normal, that was – Terence raised his eyes over the top of the book.

'Sam's party's after school. You going?'

The Gom shook his head. 'No.'

'Won't be a big party, I don't think. There'll be a model ship with presents in it.'

'For the sailors?'

The sailors? Trust the Gom to ask a Gom-like question. He closed the book, ready to go back to his own seat. The afternoon was bound to start speeding up once he was safely out of Gom-range.

Shouting goodbye to Sam and the others and saying he'd see them soon, Terence headed down Mosslands Brae. He couldn't wait to get to the party, but was in no rush to go home. Blue sky, no clouds, insects buzzing in and out of the hedge beside him, he could smell the heat rising from the tarmac road. Walking slower and slower, he dawdled to a complete stop at Robson's field, and leant against the gate to look at the cows. They were clustered together in the shade of a tree, tails flicking away the flies, their wet mouths chewing and chewing. Within seconds of his standing still, he could feel the sun start to burn into the back of his neck and his arms. He remained there for as long as he could bear it, then finally continued walking down the hill.

Bit by bit Mosslands Farm had been sold off until nothing much remained but the farmhouse and outbuildings with their peeling paintwork, rotted window frames, rusted gutters, missing slates. There was a weedy flower garden in front, a weedy vegetable garden at the back, and two small fields where sheep wandered in and out, stepping over what was left of a wooden gate. When his mother had been alive, strangers driving past sometimes thought it so 'picture-postcard-looking' they'd pull up to take photographs. Visitors had always said what a lovely house it was and how pleasant it must be to live there. Maybe if he pretended to be a visitor himself, the house would feel like it used to, and things would go better. Things had always gone better when there was a visitor.

At the turn in the road Terence crouched down and peered over the stone wall: no sign of his dad in the front garden. But sometimes he worked a bit in the vegetable patch. Keeping out of sight, he crept along to the corner and quickly looked over once more – and, yes, there was his dad's spade sticking out of the ground at the top end of a potato row, and the earth was darker from being dug recently. The yard was empty except for the tractor that hadn't moved in years and some rusted milk churns. Not a breath of wind anywhere, and heat that seemed to nail down everything.

He edged round to the other side of the house, and halted: the living-room curtains were closed. Terence knew what that meant.

But today, he reminded himself, he was going to be a visitor. He'd go in to see this lovely old 'picture-postcard' farmhouse, and this time things would be different from usual.

So…here's the visitor lifting the latch, easing the rotted frame up a good six inches to clear the long grass, and pushing the gate open enough to let himself in. Here's the visitor coming up the stone path, past the patches of overgrown lawn on either side and the thick greenery in the flowerbeds. *What a nice place this is*, thinks the visitor, *what a nice garden, what nice flowerbeds and bushes, what a nice old-fashioned pump. Never mind the dirt and dryness it coughs up, it looks really old.* The front door's for visitors, and it's not locked.

Much darker inside, cooler. In the hall Terence hesitates, one hand resting on the small wobbly table where the phone used to be. He tries his best to breathe normally. It feels like one of those days when his mother would have rushed up to him: 'Your dad's not well – best not to bother him.' Sometimes he can still hear her voice, still feel her touch.

By now, a real visitor would have lifted his hand from the table and said, 'What a nice table,' then glanced over at the grandfather clock and said, 'What a nice old grandfather clock.' If it had been years ago and his dad in a good mood, the case would have been opened to display the heavy brass pendulum swinging slowly from side to side – so slowly that its *Tick…Tick…Tick…*seemed always at the point of stopping.

The visitor pauses a couple of steps inside the living-room. With the curtains pulled shut it's difficult to see much at first, but he should take his time, visitors are always safe. *What a nice room*. In the poor light he can make out the china cabinet, the fireplace with its coal-effect electric fire in front, the TV and video. *All very nice*.

'What are you creeping around for?'

Cold-drenched to the stomach, too afraid to turn and face him, Terence tried to speak: 'I-was-just—'

'Creeping around. For what?' His dad grabbed him by the shoulder and jerked him round. 'And look at me while I'm talking.'

The sudden shove sent him stumbling backwards into one of the armchairs.

Without letting go of the chair-back Terence steadied himself. 'I was just—'

'Creeping in or creeping out – which is it?'

In the dimness his dad's face had turned angry-mad, a criss-cross of red smudges and darkness where he'd not shaved.

'I'm just in. There's Sam's party today and—'

'Just in, are you? And going straight out? That the ticket?'

Terence could feel spittle hitting his skin but knew better than to wipe it off. He took a step backwards. 'No—'

'No? But you didn't call out, did you? Didn't come round the back as usual, like you'd be expected to, did you?'

With each 'Did you?' his father took a step nearer, and he took a step further away. 'Time you learnt to behave. And till you do, you're going nowhere.'

'But Sam's party—'

'Only yourself to blame.' His father grabbed him by the shirt front. 'There's more to life than parties. Come here.'

He stepped back – and the shirt ripped.

'Now look what you've done, boy.'

A slight breeze made the late afternoon heat feel like warm breath on his shoulders. He lay quite still, face down on the field, wanting the heat to melt him away till there was nothing left. With a fistful of grass in each hand and pressing himself hard against the ground, he felt like he was holding onto planet Earth as it hurtled through empty space – holding on, but only just.

Three things: the heat, the grass, his father's rage. He had no sense of anything else and could concentrate on each one of them for only so long. It was his dad's rage that kept returning…

Finally – ten minutes? half an hour? an hour? he'd no idea – he sat up, wiped his face with a sleeve, pulled the torn shirt over his shoulder and got to his feet.

The house would be locked, of course, back door and front. All the same he knocked and shouted. He hammered at the door with his fists, kicked it. He screamed to be let in. A complete waste of time, like he knew it would be.

The village streets were empty. He walked past the church hall, the pub, the houses, cottages. No one in sight – they'd all be at Sam's party or having their tea. In some of the houses he could see people watching television while they ate. No tea for him though, and no telly – when the doors were locked at his house they stayed locked a good while.

Then he saw someone. The Gom, looking like a very lost Gom and standing in the middle of nowhere halfway down the low road.

He gave him a wave. 'How's the Gom?'

The Gom waved back and grinned. 'Hello, Terence?' More like a question, but with the Gom you could never be sure.

'It's me, all right. There's nobody else, Gom, just the two of us.' He went up to him. 'With the place empty as this, we can be aliens, like McBain was saying.'

'How do you mean?'

'Like out of a UFO, visitors from another planet.'

The Gom said nothing for a moment, then looked around him. 'I belong here.'

Trust the Gom not to get it.

'You and me, we could take over the village right now. You can have everything up to the War Memorial, and I'll have it from there to the river.'

'My gran's waiting for me.' The Gom looked closer at him. 'How come your face is all blood?'

'Don't you want to be an alien? You can come from anywhere in the universe. Anywhere you like.'

'And your shirt's ripped.'

Terence glared at him. 'See, you, Gom – you'd make a good alien. A natural. You wouldn't even have to pretend.'

'Don't you want to change it? Or get washed? You could come to my gran's and—'

'Bugger all's what I want, from you, your gran or anybody!' That was the kind of thing his dad said. 'BUGGER ALL!' he yelled, and ran away.

The back door was still locked, the living-room curtains still closed. He went round to the front – still locked as well. He was hungry and thirsty.

When he bent down and lifted the flap of the letterbox, he heard an American woman's voice saying, 'And so they should be!' – the studio audience's laughter came booming off the worn lino floor and the bare walls. He could picture his dad lying at full stretch on the couch, probably still wearing the greasy old boiler suit he never seemed to take off, the room in darkness except for the colours from the TV screen playing over him. There would be no point in knocking or shouting...or anything.

Next morning, Terence woke to the sound of rain smashing against the skylight window just above his head. He'd slept on the loft floor of the barn. Shivering, he picked the straw from his hair and face, gave his clothes a few slaps to get rid of the dust and sat up. Through the grime and cobwebs he could see low, sagging clouds and, in the distance, trees being wrenched from side to side. Over by McLeod's the corn had turned into a sea of yellow waves rushing again and again at the hedge-line, trying to break through and flood the neighbouring fields. The rain streaming down the filthy glass made everything look only half-formed: the stone dykes blackened by the wet seemed to leak into the tarmac road; the birch trees along the river were tangled up with running water one moment, then blown into the sky the next. A real storm.

He got to his feet and brushed the worst of the straw from his clothes. A few moments later he'd climbed down the ladder and charged across the yard in the pouring rain, making for the back door. It was open.

The house was silent except for over by the cooker where a leak splashed onto the lino every couple of seconds. *Drip...Drip... Drip...*He washed his face at the kitchen tap and was drying himself on a tea-towel when he suddenly caught sight of his father through the window. Out in the pouring rain, and not wearing a coat or anything, just the usual boiler suit – he was standing quite still, his hands resting on the spade as if he couldn't decide whether to start digging or not.

Who cared what his dad was doing? While keeping watch out the kitchen window, Terence bolted down a Mars bar and a butter sandwich, then took several large gulps of water straight from the tap. From a heap of clothes lying on the floor waiting to be washed he took a sweatshirt.

Breakfast over, he grabbed his denim jacket and left.

At school everyone was talking about Sam's party and asking why he hadn't been there.

He had his answers ready. 'My dad needed me…I was busy… There's more to life than parties.'

Sam had brought him his Lucky Dip present from out of the ship – he said thank you and stuffed it in his pocket to open later.

All morning while McBain's voice droned on and on and on he kept thinking about his dad, picturing him as he'd seen him earlier: standing in the vegetable garden, gripping the spade handle like it was the helm of an old-fashioned ship, and looking like a captain fighting to stay afloat in the middle of a storm. The deck was a pitching, sliding mass of rain, earth, long grass, broken branches, bushes, torn leaves.

It was during paired reading with the Gom – he hardly listened, and when it was his turn he just read into himself – that Terence suddenly realised what he had to do: he would invite the Gom to his house over lunchtime, the first visitor they'd had in years. With a visitor, everything was always all right.

The Gom said no, his mum was expecting him home and she'd be worried. She got really worried if he was only five minutes late even.

Let her know then. Sam lived next door to the Gom, and could tell his mum he'd be a bit late. No problem.

But she'd have made something for his lunch and if he didn't—

For just some of lunchtime then? He wanted him to come, it would be good fun, the two of them.

The Gom wasn't happy. He sat and sat and said nothing, and seemed to be sweating more than ever.

Terence stood at the bottom of Mosslands Brae, outside his house. He was so hungry. The rain hadn't stopped all morning and was now coming down harder than ever. He'd edge round the side of the house to check if the curtains were closed. With a bit of luck his dad might be out at the post office or getting something from the shop.

'Terence?'

His mother? Standing right behind him?

'Terence?'

Because of the rain he hadn't heard her coming. Then her touch at his sleeve...

Ready to throw himself into her arms, he whirled round.

'You! What are you doing here, Gom?'

'I-was—'

'You were creeping around.'

'I've come like you asked. Not for long. But you asked me, people don't ask...not much.'

Terence gave him a grin.

The Gom grinned back showing his teeth and gums.

Because he was with a visitor today, there'd be no need for crouching down and peering over the wall and so Terence marched straight into the garden. Ignoring the driving rain he pointed out the lawn, the flowers, the old pump. Tour of the garden over, they went into the dim hall and stood in front of the old grandfather clock. The Gom kept nodding and smiling. Terence opened the case to let him see the pendulum.

'Needs wound up,' he explained.

Where was his dad? He wanted him to know they had a visitor, then maybe he'd be friendly like he'd sometimes been before... offer them lemonade...wind up the clock so they could watch the pendulum swing backwards and forwards like it used to, and hear it tick.

His dad wasn't in the living-room either. They looked at the china cabinet, the coal-effect electric fire, then went through to the kitchen.

'I wanted you to meet my dad.'

'Seen him before, in the village, in the shop, seen him loads of times and—'

After they'd dried themselves off on the tea-towel, Terence poured some lemonade and got out the packet of Mars bars. The Gom kept complaining he'd have to be getting home soon, his mum would be wondering where he was. Thanks for the lemonade and the chocolate, but he really had to go.

'There's something else I want to show you, something really special! Something secret!'

The Gom looked desperate. 'Have to go.'

'Only take a few minutes, Gom. Honest.'

Terence led the way out to the back garden. First he walked up the path and pointed to the different vegetables, shouting to be heard above the wind and driving rain.

'These are potatoes…onions…peas…cabbages…carrots…'

When they reached the end of the rows there was only a foot of grass remaining, then came the stone dyke.

The Gom pulled at his arm. 'Have to go. Have to go.'

'See this spade?' Terence began. 'Well, remember Sam's party?' He smiled. 'The ship you heard about? And the hold with the Lucky Dip and everything? Well, instead of putting presents in a ship, my dad's buried them for us here in the garden. For you and me, and when we—'

The Gom was already running back down the path. 'Getting late, getting late.'

'But you've got to stay, don't—'

The spade lifted easily out of the ground. Seemed light as a feather almost as Terence raised it, swung it above his head, aimed in the direction of the vanishing Gom.

Then hurled it as hard as he could.

The clang the metal made hitting the cement path felt like a blow in the face. Terence staggered back against the dyke. He felt so very, very cold. Chilled suddenly, as if he'd never get warm again.

His father was standing at the back door, looking more angry-mad than ever.

Terence knew this time was going to be the worst. The very worst. Slowly he walked towards him. 'Dad, there's been a visitor.'

His father said nothing.

'A visitor. He's gone now. I showed him the house like we used to. The pump, the clock, the kitchen, the vegetable garden. I gave him something to drink and a Mars bar.'

'What the hell are you talking about?'

'He needed looking after, the visitor. Been out in the rain and everything. Needed looking after.'

'No visitors wanted in this house, no bugger-all wanted. Just you. Get yourself inside.'

Not wanting to risk being hit, Terence ran past him through the doorway. 'Dad—'

'Visitor, my arse.'

'He said – he said to say hello to you.'

In the kitchen it was even darker than before, and cold. Rain was gusting hard against the window. His dad sat down.

Terence knew he had to keep talking. 'You're soaked as well, just like him, like the visitor.' He pushed the tea-towel within reach. It was ignored. Rainwater continued running off his dad's hands onto the table.

He had to do something. Anything.

Having dug in his pocket he pulled out the present Sam had given him at school. 'The visitor – he left this, said it was for you.'

'What are you on about?'

'A Lucky Dip prize. For you. It's special.' Terence put the

sellotaped packet, red-wrapped with stuck-on gold stars, on the table. 'I'd better be getting back to the school. You can open it, if you like.'

'Lucky Dip?' His father picked up the small package and began turning it over and over in his wet hands. 'What the fuck do I want with a Lucky Dip?'

Like he'd never seen a present before, thought Terence as he edged further away; like it was something that had dropped from the skies.

He grabbed his jacket and rushed out of the house.

Having made his way across the yard he stopped at the gate, then turned to look back at the house. He was getting drenched through, but still he stood there. Rainwater gushed out of the leaking rones and gutters to go splashing down the stonework of the house; from the sheds came the scrape and screech of corrugated iron being wrenched loose by the wind; the front garden was turning into mud.

Suddenly Terence shouted. 'He was an alien, the visitor – and he's gone back to his own planet. One look at this place was enough for him!'

He started laughing. Next moment he was marching through the wind and rain up the road to school, stamping through the puddles, swinging his arms at his sides and yelling at the very top of his voice: 'LUCKY DIP!...WHAT THE FUCK!...LUCKY DIP!... WHAT THE FUCK!'

Five fantastic fictions

I. A visit to the oracle

The Delphic Oracle was having a bad day. Outside, Mediterranean sunlight was bleaching the vineyards and hillsides and shimmering on the cobalt-blue Aegean. Inside, in the dimness of the sacred cave, the queue of punters seeking her advice in the form of riddles and enigmas seemed never-ending: shepherds and kings, 5-star generals and multinational CEOs. The holy incense was making her eyes water; her head-dress of writhing snakes was a disaster; each divine utterance was becoming more enigmatic than the last. Her cave needed a makeover it would never get. She needed a break.

Next up was a politician who had turned sincerity into a brand-name stamped across his forehead. Though he had planned to present himself as a humble supplicant, PR demanded an entourage of men with mobile phones, and Security demanded a team of armed guards who swept the cave (only electronically, the priestess was disappointed to note) for weapons and bugs. For everyone's comfort and security the skies were dark with helicopters.

'If *we* are not in control,' explained this champion of world democracy, 'the entire world will be out of control.'

Where have I heard that before? the priestess thought to herself. Just then, one of the writhing snakes slid from her head-dress, glided miraculously through the sacred fire, slithered up close to the People's Representative, and bit him. So engrossed was he in the truth of what he was saying, however, that he didn't feel a thing.

Back in his own country, he addressed his Cabinet. Being brave, he said nothing about that rather nippy itch on his ankle. It was business as usual. No rest for the righteous, was his motto.

Halfway through the meeting he began talking in riddles and enigmas. No one noticed the difference. The result was droughts, disease and famines, terror and free-market investment. Shares were bought and sold. Aid parcels and cluster bombs fell. Some cities were liberated, some became rubble. Life went on, and death.

2. The colourful life of Calum McCall

During the early years of his life, Calum McCall was surprised to find himself waking up every morning in a winter country of darkened tenements, black railings and streets of pitiless traffic. There seemed to be only one sun in the Scottish sky, and it wasn't even striped – which perhaps explained the look of perpetual disappointment he could see in the faces of the men and women who lived there.

Every so often he tried asking his parents: 'What has happened to the multicoloured suns that used to bounce across the sky, and to the colours that trailed after like rain?'

'Aye right,' said his dad.

'Elbows off the table,' said his mother.

At school his teacher told him to sit up straight and pay attention – that way he would get ahead.

When he fell in love for the first time he told the girl – she was called Alice – that her kisses brought back all the colours he had known so early on, and which were now faded almost to nothing in his memory. Alice said he was sweet, and a few months later she got engaged to an up-and-coming dentist.

Years later, Calum married and had children of his own. One day his baby son pointed at the sky and gurgled with pleasure. Calum followed the pointing finger, but could see nothing particularly special up there – nothing that was visible to him, anyway.

That night he slept badly for the first time.

Now that he was in a position of responsibility, he could not afford to turn up at his office dishevelled with lack of sleep, not among his ambitious colleagues. His doctor gave him a packet of brightly coloured pills.

Every morning now, Calum is up early, ready for the day ahead. Every night, he slips from one utterly dreamless world into the next.

3. A glitch in the universe

On the evening before his tenth birthday young William Littlejohn stood at his bedroom window and saw the falling star. He closed his eyes and made a wish.

Twenty years later, the brand-new bicycle he'd asked for shimmered into substantiality during a merger meeting. Mr Lofthouse, the chairman, lost the attention of his fellow-board members as, right in front of their very eyes, a gleaming chrome frame complete with wheels, pedals, chain, handlebars, bell, mirror and wheel-stabilisers began slowly emerging out of thin air to become the centrepiece of the boardroom table. A bright red 'whirrer' was attached to the spokes.

Lofthouse demanded to know what the game was?

The ice-cold sweat of denied responsibility ran down the inside of junior executive Littlejohn's tailored shirt. Security was called and, as the bike was wheeled away down the corridor, its whirrer seemed to call plaintively to him.

That night Littlejohn didn't sleep a wink.

In time, he was promoted to junior partner: new office, new secretary, new view, new washroom. As he stared out over the city, he almost believed that the sunbeams on the adjacent glass skyscrapers were dancing just for him.

Over the next year a retriever puppy, a dune buggy and a real-life Miss February centrefold were among a series of startling and embarrassing materialisations. Clearly there was a glitch in the universe – his adolescent wishes were being granted, but too late.

The young executive became gaunt from sleeplessness. He married, had children, moved to a good neighbourhood. Nothing seemed to help.

One morning he found himself seated at the chairman's desk. Funny, he couldn't remember wishing to actually *become* old Lofthouse, but there he was…and – ah yes! – he could recognise his former boss in the new junior partner, sharpening company pencils down at the bottom of the boardroom table.

Just then Security burst in, accompanied by the police. They approached, flourished documents. Bandied about were words like 'embezzlement', 'insider-trading', 'jail'. As he was led away, Littlejohn was quite certain he saw the new junior glance up, catch his eye and wink at him.

4. Moses's little brother

The day after Moses and the Twelve Tribes of Israel set off into the wilderness, his little brother ran up to the head of the procession.

'We'll be out of here in no time – I have a map.'

Big Brother, of course, knew better. After all, God was on their side, and not just any god, of which there were plenty in those far-off generous days, but the one true God – He who could provide plagues of locusts, frogs and boils, and could part the Red Sea when required.

'No, thank you,' Moses replied, 'We have a cloud by day and a pillar of fire by night. We don't need maps.'

'But it'll tell us—'

'When God wants to tell us anything, he'll turn into a burning bush.'

That night, after Moses and the Twelve Tribes had hurried off to catch up with the pillar of fire, Little Brother shrugged and lay down in the sand. Next thing, God was shaking him.

'You're on your own!' came the Divine warning.

'Suits me.' He turned over, and went back to sleep.

A few days later, Moses's little brother reached the Promised Land. Milk and honey for those with work permits – but for the likes of him, it was either the building-site or delivering pizzas…

The Twelve Tribes showed up forty years later. There was a

dispute. Several other gods, both local and freelance, got involved and, three thousand years after that, everyone was still at it. A partition was followed by refugee camps, suicide-bombers, missiles. Someone produced a new map. Someone started building a wall.

God turned Himself into a burning bush. No one noticed.

'Okay,' He said, 'no more Mr Nice Guy,' and reached for his Book of Plagues. The updated version.

5. Schoenberg and
The Sandman

Like everyone else at the end of the nineteenth century, Arnold Schoenberg, the great composer and music theorist, took his seat on the crowded train heading towards an ever-better world. After turning the corner into the glorious future ahead, the engine started picking up speed – only to go slamming into a solid wall.

Bits went everywhere: bits of countries, bits of colonies, bits of science, art and religion. The tracks, seeming to stretch back to the beginnings of Time, were wrenched apart; buckled and bent, they clawed at the blue skies above Passchendaele, Ypres, Flanders.

Suddenly, the streets were full of people who knew best. Their self-appointed task: to get civilisation back on the rails. They all agreed that drastic problems need drastic solutions – and each had a solution more drastic than the one before.

On all sides, there began such a noise of hammering and welding, such a clamour and din of revolution, extermination, colonial expansion and unemployment; of mass production and racial purity. The Stock Exchange boomed, the trains were made to run on time.

Schoenberg, meanwhile, had decided to discard tonality. He declared that his new discovery – the twelve-tone system – would create harmonic possibilities strong enough to hold everything together. Even chaos itself.

Around him, the streets bustled with strikers and strike-breakers; financiers went thudding onto pavements; cattle trucks began criss-crossing Europe. There were parades, searchlights, flags, roaring ovens, transatlantic sailings to the sound of restaurant orchestras. There was reasoned debate and orderly soup queues.

Soon Schoenberg was rushing up to complete strangers. 'My twelve-tone system offers real value for money to composer, player and audience alike.'

Once all the lights of Europe had gone out, The Sandman tiptoed from country to country tucking the sleepers tight in their beds. That done, he began telling them their dreams. Schoenberg closed his eyes believing the time would come when mothers crooned his twelve-tone lullabies to their children. This particular dream made even The Sandman smile.

Alice Kerr went with older men

I

In less than two minutes he'd be in Environmental Studies. In less than two minutes he'd be sitting next to Alice Kerr. Steve's whole body went rigid. All-over lust. He could feel himself shaking. Teeth gritted, fists clenched, toes curled. What a fucking life! Steve Merrick – the Fifth Year Virgin…and the only known virgin left in the whole class, barring his friend Billy.

He stared out the boys' locker room window: he had to think about something else, something depressing. Quick. The bell was about to ring. Something really depressing: Scotland's not qualifying for the World Cup? Those planes going into the Twin Towers? Blair? Bush? The Iraq War? The melting ice caps? The threatened rainforests?

Anything but Alice Kerr; her long black hair, her short black skirt, her slow sexy smile.

He shut his eyes: *the Twin Towers, the threatened rainforests…*

Alice Kerr went with older men. She'd been seen in the back of a bus, the driver and one of the passengers having her at the same time. At the Tollbridge Terminus.

A wee first year was sticking his finger up one of the taps to make the water spray out – Steve glared at him to stop.

The bell rang.

As he leant forward to pick up his Adidas bag from the shelf behind the washbasins, *it* touched the porcelain rim. He caught his breath and remained there: teeth gritted, fists clenched, toes curled. *The threatened rainforests, the threatened rainforests.*

'Steve?' His friend Billy was calling him from the doorway. 'You coming?'

'It's just the way I'm standing.' The classic reply.

He turned round. If he stopped thinking about Alice Kerr, and if he kept his bag in front of him, maybe no one would notice. Crossing the hall and going up the stairs, he concentrated on every Alice-Kerr-free detail of Billy's tale of experimenting with a cider-and-stout mixture the night before.

'Called Black Velvet. Five pints in the station buffet, then straight out and I'm heaving it over the tracks. Tell you, Steve, five pints is a fair load when you see it all at once.'

Into the classroom. Alice Kerr was already there, less than half a metre between her seat and his.

He managed to sit down without staring at her, nearly. She didn't look in his direction, but then she never did. He tried to get interested in a wall-poster about Third World Poverty, then one about soil erosion, then some blow-up pictures illustrating global warming. Alice Kerr put the tip of her pencil into her mouth. She began sucking on it.

His toes curled again.

She turned towards him. 'Want a photo?'

'No, I was just—'

But she'd already prodded the girl next to her: 'I thought he fancied me, but he says he doesn't want a photo. Not very gallant, eh Kirsty?'

Steve was going red, he could feel it. A real fucking beamer.

'Oh, him!' Kirsty Thing was staring straight at him. 'Doesn't know when he's well-off. Likely gets on better with photos, that one. A slow developer, right enough!'

He turned away and pretended to be interested in what Haggis-head was saying.

'Today we'll be considering Continental Plates…'

Another eight and a half months until summer. Thirty-four more weeks of being stuck in a classroom in Nowhere, Scotland: getting himself qualified enough to sign on. Most of his classmates knew what they fancied signing on as: Billy as a web-designer; Alice Kerr and Kirsty Thing were going into tourism. The Einsteins in the smart row were going on to college; his own row was headed straight for early retirement – better that, at least, than going for a soldier these days. But he must have missed a lesson sometime in the last five years, the one where everyone learnt who they were.

Haggis-head was drizzling on about 'faults'. On his desk at the front was a brightly coloured plastic mountain that wasn't the least bit Scottish-looking; amazing he hadn't tried swapping it for a tartan one. Half the coloured bits of the mountain slipped when there was a 'fault'. According to Haggis-head the Earth's surface kept moving all the time. *Continental Plates* was chalked up on the board along with a whole swirl of red and green arrows and numbers. To his right Billy was doing his best to get some sleep; to his left Alice Kerr had already started on her own swirl of red and green arrows. Over two hundred days to go, with Alice Kerr sitting next to him in every Environmental Studies class and him getting harder by the minute. A gigantic stiffie eight and a half months long.

Nearly an hour till they got out, then it was The Causes of the Second World War for another hour. All his life he'd been sitting in one classroom or another while someone went on about Continental Plates, or the potato, Winston Churchill, or whales, *Hamlet*…

'Perhaps Merrick will explain this phenomenon to us more clearly. It seems so familiar to him that he needs take no notice of what I'm saying.'

Shit! Haggis-head was claiming him.

'Well, Merrick. The incidence of shift in the San Andreas Fault – your observations?'

His what?

'Or were you too busy observing the young lady to your left, perhaps?' A smarmy-looking smile towards Alice Kerr. 'A most pardonable *fault*.' Another smarmy smile, then turning back to him with the smile switched off. 'But not in my class!'

Alice Kerr and Kristy Thing were staring at him, grinning. He clenched his fists under the desk. Another fucking beamer, the second in five minutes. Sweat had started trickling down the back of his shirt.

'We're waiting, Merrick.'

The dickhead was likely to be waiting a long time yet: never mind the answer, what was the fucking question? Not that it mattered, except that Haggis-head was a bampot-dickhead, and Alice Kerr would be thinking he was too. It was school that did it. There should be a Government Health Warning stamped on Haggis-head's forehead: 'SCHOOL DAMAGES YOU FOR LIFE'. Steve wanted out. OUT, before he got so stiff he was having to pogo-stick everywhere. All he had to do was get to his feet and leave. He'd even give them a short farewell-speech: 'Environmental Studies—' and he'd point to the posters and the plastic mountain, 'Environmental Studies – or LIFE!' They'd be gob-smacked, the lot of them. Alice Kerr would sit gazing after him in wonder and admiration. He'd give her one last look from the doorway: heroic, yet tinged with sadness and longing for what might have been. Haggis-head would sit holding his head in his hands, regretting his life wasted as an Environmental Studies dickhead, its pointlessness, its—

'On your feet, boy, when you're answering a question.'

'But I've not said anything yet.' He'd spoken before he could stop himself.

'A comedian, eh?' Haggis-head was charging towards him. The dickhead's spittle showered his face and, close to, the birthmark on his cheek was like a wound that hadn't healed properly.

'Look at me, boy.'

Steve looked.

'You're here to work, not to play the comic. Not to drool over young ladies, no matter how charming they may be.' Another smarmy smile for Alice Kerr. 'Not to daydream. You understand? To work. Work. Understand?'

'Yes.' *Dickhead.*

'Yes...?'

'Yes, sir.'

Yes, dickhead. No, dickhead. Up yours, dickhead.

'Now pay attention.'

Haggis-head went back to his plastic mountain and began labouring his way through another demonstration of a fault. This time he shouted, 'CRASH!' when the layers slipped, making the rest of the class laugh out loud. Fucking hyenas.

Steve opened his jotter, gripped his green pencil and began colouring in.

For the next quarter of an hour he carried on as best he could: trying not to look over at Alice Kerr, trying not to think about Alice Kerr. Trying not to think about *anything*...Maybe, when the great day came – that great and glorious day when he'd finally lose his virginity – then the world would seem a wonderful place. A place of permanent celebration where sex was everywhere, and every girl would want...

NO. NO. NO.

He had to stop thinking about it. He *had* to.

But until that day came…how could he last out? How could he possibly last out? How? How?

All at once he threw down his pencil in horror. What the hell had he been doing? He'd forgotten all about the fault marks and drawn a completely green mountain, green from top to bottom: an ordinary mountain, not an Environmental Studies one. Now what? Start all over again, or make it really ordinary instead, really Scottish?

He picked up a clutch of coloured pencils and began scribbling. He'd call it 'Concept Scotland – The Tartan Experience'. He was inspired. This was going to be a mountain to die for: a derelict castle, some stags, some Highlanders with kilts and claymores, a few tourists with Alice Kerr and Kirsty Thing showing them around. A bit of blue for a loch, a few green and orange spots for Nessie's head, black for a slag-heap, and a hairy cow, brown. That looked more like it! Some football supporters, more blue, with a bubble chanting 'Scotland! Scotland!' An oil rig, a sub and stickmen for Faslane and the demonstrators, a big round-looking tower with red sparks shooting out of it for a nuclear reactor. Two guys leaning against the slag-heap like they were having a pint, a wee turret for the sub in the loch, extra scribble for rain. Was that the lot? Some jerky-looking zigzags and curved bits for the New Parliament, and a bit more rain, maybe. Where should he put himself? With the supporters? With the guys getting pissed? Giving a speech at the Parliament, or doing a highland fling on the turret?

Haggis-head was still droning on and next year's dole queue was still taking notes. Steve laid down his pencil. Drawing mountains? On days like this he could fucking hardly even draw breath. Alice Kerr was busy adding a multicoloured statistical chart to her details of the San Andreas Fault. Could she really have had it away with two people at the same time?

Seconds later he was hard again.

The threatened rainforests. World poverty. Global warming.
The Twin Towers. Iraq.
Whales.

He was going to end up rigid for life. Soon he'd be hanging around supermarket carparks and dark alleys in an old raincoat. He had to stop thinking about Alice Kerr. He had to stop spending his life trying not to think about Alice Kerr.

Alice Kerr was looking over at him. She was smiling at him.

Fuck!

She was tucking a lock of hair behind her ear, now she was leaning towards him.

Fuck! Fuck! *It* would be lifting the desk off the floor any minute. Maybe she'd tell Kirsty Thing. Give her a good laugh: then the two of them'd be texting everyone – *Steve Merrick, class pervert.*

'Hm…' she smiled.

If she leant any closer *it* would be bursting through.

'Hm…' Her low, sexy voice. 'You'll not want Haggis-head to catch you with that.' Another smile. 'But I like it.'

She liked it? Fuck's sake, was that what she'd said? She leant any nearer and there'd be nothing left of him but a smear on the seat.

He gripped the edge of the desk, stared down hard at his green mountain: *The threatened rainforests. The threatened rainforests.*

'The castle most of all, but d'you not want a wee flag on it, maybe?'

The period dragged. And·dragged. Meanwhile he could see a clear autumn day out there in the real world. Steve watched a guy walking his collie dog in the playing-fields, throwing sticks for it. Lucky guy. Lucky dog. Lucky stick.

'For these are my mountains, or are they?' Haggis-head was off again. 'The New Scottish Parliament they call it, and *where* d'you think it's got us?'

'Craigbar.' He heard Billy whisper.

'New Scottish Parliament!' The dickhead was getting himself stoked up. 'I'll tell you what that is: a bunch of Oor Wullies, Wee McGreegors, Peter Pans and Tinkerbells. Hardly a grown-up in the place. Wains wi their Whitehall faither!'

Haggis-head's face had gone so red with anger the birthmark had almost disappeared, the danger signal was when it vanished altogether. That was when someone would be getting themselves a bad time. So long as it wasn't him.

Haggis-head stopped in mid-sentence, then wrote *San Andreas Fault* on the blackboard, breaking the chalk twice.

Now for the mad glare, starting at the right-hand side of the class:

'So, where exactly is the San Andreas Fault?'

No response.

Mad glare along the left-hand side:

'The San Andreas Fault, come on?'

No response.

'I'll be kind to you. I'll give you a clue. The answer is California.' A pause. 'Or Kansas.' Another pause. 'Now, which is it?'

Still no response. They weren't Kamikazes.

Mad glare along the first row. 'Hardly a difficult question. Even the dimmest has a fifty per cent chance of getting it right.'

Mad glare along the second row. 'Or wrong.'

Another pause.

Then the final mad glare, a real wall-eyed job taking in the whole class at once. 'Let's get the right answer this time, not like your parents did back in '79.'

What was Haggis-head on about? 1979? He'd not even been born then.

'Paterson?'

Silence.

'Hastings?'

Silence.

'Third time lucky…' The mad glare was homing in on the third row, his. Each desk in turn: Lorraine Thing, Kirsty Thing, Alice Kerr…

'Ah, our fault expert, Mr Steve Merrick.'

The bastard. It wasn't fair. He'd done his bit already.

'Have a guess, Merrick.'

'Mmmm.'

'Yes?'

He was on his own now: one to one, him and Haggis-head. The rest of the class wanting him to fuck it up so *he'd* be the one getting screamed at, and not them. They'd get entertained.

'Yes, Merrick?'

'Kan—'

He should stop there and wait for the reaction.

'Kan-?' The dickhead was prompting him, creepy-polite.

He'd try the other one. 'Cal—'

'Speak up, boy!'

Cal or Kan? He'd no idea and didn't give a fuck anyway. Haggis-head was just baiting him, enjoying himself.

'Kan—' Steve shrugged, '—sas.'

He waited. Several seconds passed.

Haggis-head's silence was like the mountain he'd shown them earlier, before it had crashed apart.

Then it came.

'Merrick, you're a stupid, stupid, stupid boy. You're an idiot. A moron!'

The rest of the class was a wall-to-wall grin.

Beamer number three, a full-stretcher that Steve could feel searing its way from the crown of his head to the very tips of his toes. He stared down at the desk.

Fuck. Fuck. Fuck.

When the bell rang at the end of the period Steve stood up. Alice Kerr didn't even glance in his direction.

He turned to Billy. 'I'm off, see you later.'

He started towards the door.

He heard Haggis-head calling him. 'Merrick, you've left your books behind.'

Without breaking his stride he called back over his shoulder, 'Right enough, sir,' and kept on going. Through the door, down the corridor. The Causes of the Second World War were coming next, but not for him.

2

The following morning Steve was putting the finishing touches to his new image in the bathroom mirror. Here was *the man*: the man with a mission, the man to keep the wheels of Britain turning. Clean hair, clean denim shirt and clean second-best jeans in case they wanted him to start immediately. He'd try some sites first. Demolition and unemployment were the two growth industries these days. It was either that or becoming an MSP and voting himself another pay-rise. HA-HA-FUCKING-HA!

The man with a mission laughed back at him.

He'd start with the site behind the railway where the old cottage hospital was being bulldozed into rubble to make way for a new supermarket. That, or somewhere else. He'd have a job by lunchtime no problem and be a couple of hundred quid up by the weekend. Then he'd give Alice Kerr the time of her life. Billy and co. would be enjoying double French this morning, with double maths for afters; and getting a Modern Studies test in the afternoon. A big grin from mission-man, and the thumbs up:

'Nice one!'

In the kitchen his mother was standing by the back door, putting on her coat ready to go off to her job at B&Q. She wasn't smiling.

'There's some tea in the pot. I'm away. I'll speak to McIver to see if there's anything. Your dad'll be up by ten, mind.'

Meaning: if you've any sense you'll be out the house by ten.

'Right, Mum. Thanks.'

'Don't get your hopes up about McIver. I'll be just asking, that's all.'

Meaning: she'll be looking out for a job for him so he'd better be doing the same. He told her he'd already got a list of places to try. Quick tea and toast, then out to the cottage hospital, or the road widening, or the new houses down by the river.

She still wasn't smiling. 'See you tonight then.'

'If I'm not back for my tea, I'll be on overtime!' He waved her out the door.

Eight forty-five on the cooker clock: a relaxed breakfast catching up on the football in yesterday's paper. This was the life.

They'd be in registration now: rows of stookies getting their names ticked off, getting told to take their bags off the desks, not to wear their jackets in class, not to move until the bell. Billy'd be crapping himself over a history project he'd not even started yet. History – HA-HA-FUCKING-HA! His own desk near the door, empty – the one that got away. In registration Alice Kerr sat over by the window: he'd had a good think about her once already in bed this morning, he could go a second one now for luck. He'd finish the football, then nip upstairs for a quick pretend that Alice Kerr was wanting him to...

Fuck. That was the toilet flushing. His dad, and it wasn't even nine.

Onto his feet and into overdrive: trainers on, grab his jacket and out. Closing the door quiet as quiet – or his dad'd come battering down the stairs, yelling after him.

Most of the cottage hospital was still needing knocked down. The back and side walls of the main building were waiting to be finished off: broken bedframes, mattresses, doors, bricks and smashed cupboards were piled into a heap the size of two or three houses, and waiting to be carried away. Plenty of work. There was rubble everywhere, with planks of wood laid over puddles and holes in the ground where the electric wiring stuck out like multi-coloured weeds. Only a couple of people seemed to be on-site: a fat man in a yellow hard hat was revving up a dumper truck while a tall, sleepy-looking guy stood and watched.

Stepping on a board marked OUT-PATIENTS Steve went over to them.

'Hello.'

Yellow-hat kept revving. Sleepy-eyes kept standing and watching.

The motor was too loud for talking over. He stood and watched too. Maybe if he stood and watched long enough he'd get paid as well.

'Try giving it some more,' shouted Sleepy-eyes.

Yellow-hat gave it some more.

The motor roared to breaking point. Then broke.

Yellow-hat slapped his hand on the wheel. 'That's that well and truly fucked then. I'll not be needing a driver any more, will I?' He climbed down from the seat.

Sleepy-eyes took a step back. 'It wasn't me.'

'Never is. *Me* never does anything. Plenty I's in this country: *I* want, *I* need, *I* get – but fuck all Me's doing fuck all.' He turned to Steve: 'And which are you, son – an *I* or a *Me*?'

'I was hoping to get a job, a start.'

'"*I* hope" – that's another one. A start is it? Can you start dumpers with broken motors?'

'Mmm.'

'Have you got a few thousand to ease my cash-flow?'

He'd come at a bad time. 'There's nothing?'

Yellow-hat spread his arms wide to take in the heaps of rubble. 'Top of the fucking class, son.' Then he walked away, disappearing round the side of a half-demolished wall.

Sleepy-eyes shrugged and disappeared after him.

Quite alone now, Steve gazed around at what was left of the hospital. Some sheets of paper tacked to a noticeboard were set rustling by the wind; a door that was marked DISPENSARY and led nowhere swung open and banged shut every few seconds. It was going to rain soon and there was no roof. He left.

He tried the new supermarket. Nothing. Come back around Xmas.

The road widening – nothing. The new houses – nothing.

He took a short cut through the old railway station with its boarded-up windows and lead-free roof – all that was left now was the Station Buffet, the underage hangout where if you could reach up to the bar you got served. If his dad still worked as a shunter driver, he'd have got a start in the sheds himself. Not now though. Even though he felt sorry for the old man, he couldn't help looking on him as an adult-sized warning of how not to plan your life.

A walk downtown to check out the High Street. The only people about were a few job-seekers passing the time by throwing a torn bag of chips at each other. Entertainment Craigbar-style.

Midday. He was standing outside the Post Office, and getting soaked. Back at the ranch his dad would be sitting reading the paper, or else just sitting. He could sit with him. Or stay where he was. In the rain.

A right fucking morning that had been.

Lunchtime with his dad seemed to make his first day of freedom drag even slower than a schoolday.

His brief update on his job progress so far was followed by a long, long silence while the two of them finished their cheese-on-toast and listened to the rain hammering against the kitchen window. The radio talked to itself about Iraqi suicide bombers, about American marines, about the democratic process. There was a steady *drip-drip* of condensation onto the windowsill. On Friday nights they'd always had a late tea when his dad, a few pints inside him, would sit pissed and cheerful until about nine. One moment he'd be joking with them and the next – in mid-sentence even – the week's tiredness would hit him all at once, like he was being mugged. He'd stop talking, a few seconds' pause – then wallop! He'd stay like that without speaking for a bit longer, then drag himself upstairs to bed and not be seen till Saturday lunchtime. That 'mugged' expression had stuck ever since he'd been laid off, and today he appeared even more mugged-looking than usual against the background of rain, condensation and government foreign policy.

'Would the teacher not have you back?' His dad directed his question at the empty space between the fridge and the cooker.

'He might do, but for what? Come next summer it'll be no different. Worse even as there'll be more folk trying for a start, and all at the same time.'

A right idiot he'd look going back now. His dad was hardly listening though, and a few minutes later had gone through to watch *Neighbours*. Alice Kerr and Kirsty Thing watched *Neighbours*. A few days and he'd be doing it too, would he? And at lunchtime?

He washed the dishes, then tramped round town all afternoon.

Asda, Comet, a timberyard, two more building sites. Nothing...
nothing...nothing...nothing. Nothing.

His mum came home. There was nothing at B&Q either. Maybe
around Xmas, doing temporary work.

Better if he just took to his bed till Xmas – seemed that was
when it was all happening.

He was up and out the house before nine the following morning.
Back for lunch. He stayed in the kitchen to avoid *Neighbours*, but
heard it booming word for word through the wall. Then out again:
a talk with some guys digging up the road – nothing. The Post
Office – nothing. The Job Centre – plenty leaflets, but no jobs. The
library to check out the papers – nothing.

Back home the TV was still on. His dad had been watching it
nearly all day, like most days in the last few years. His own dad –
glued to *Sunset Beach*, *Des and Mel*, *Countdown* and to that endless
Home-Makeover shite. His own dad.

It was past four. Having scrunched up 'Choosing the Right Job
– the Choice is Yours' and the rest of the handouts about services,
products and strategies, and filed them in the bin, he sat at the
kitchen table reading the football for the second time. His tea had
gone cold.

There was a knock on the window.

Billy was white-nosed against the glass. He got up to let him
in.

'Not a bad life eh, Steve? Some of us have just had forty minutes
on the digestion of the dogfish,' he laughed. 'So, how's it going?'

'Piece of piss. Seat?'

'No thanks. Fancy a stroll down the burn? I heard Alice Kerr
might just be passing that way.'

'Why should I care?'

Had Alice Kerr actually told Billy she'd be there?

Not *exactly*, it seemed. But the possibility was worth a quick wash and brush up while Billy waited downstairs. Then test the breath, test the plooks. Thumbs-up all round.

Five minutes later they cut through a gap in the back hedge and were scrambling down the slope.

Billy jumped the last stretch and landed beside him on the tarmac. 'Skitey, that. Wonder they let people slide down it.'

The two of them started walking along the burn path.

'Some exit, Steve. "Merrick, you've left your books." "Right enough, sir." That was telling the tartan bampot. Ten out of ten for style!'

But what had Alice Kerr made of it? He wouldn't ask though. Stay cool.

'Haggis-head hung himself in despair yet?'

'More likely to be hanging you. Him shouting "Merrick! Merrick!" down the corridor, and you not giving a shit. Christ, he was mad.'

But…Alice Kerr?

'He told Four-eyes to get your books and put them on his desk.'

'Man's a fucking balloon.'

Even if Alice Kerr hadn't said anything she must have thought something. She might be showing up at any minute. Maybe now that he'd left school she realised what she was missing?

'Four-eyes is sitting next to her now.'

'Next to who?'

'You know fine who. Waste of a good seat: specs like glass bricks on him and Alice Kerr's probably still just a blur.'

After they'd walked the next half dozen yards in silence he asked, as casually as he could, 'She's coming down the burn, you say?'

'So rumour has it.'

A few yards further on Billy turned to him.

'Anyway, how's it going? Any jobs?'

They'd come to the big question. What was he going to say? Two days of nothing with more nothing to come? That he was not watching *Neighbours* at least? He stopped walking and stood in the middle of the path.

'Jobs? You must be fucking joking. Take a good look round. On the left, what have we? The closed-up railway station. To the right, ladies and gentlemen: the cottage hospital that's so out of cash it can't afford to get itself knocked down even. Straight ahead: the town cemetery. Let me tell you, Billy boy, the casual alien visiting Craigbar would see no visible signs of life, and a closer inspection would reveal there fucking isn't any.'

He carried on walking. 'But I've a few ideas up for consideration.'

'Aye, like what?'

They were coming out of the small glen near to where the park proper started. The bowling green and tennis courts were up ahead. Usually they were run by old guys who spent all their time banning folk. Come spring he could try there; *he* wouldn't ban anyone.

'Well, like starting my own business.'

'Aye, like what?'

'You're turning into a record, Billy. Too much school's what does that. Nowadays you want a job you've got to start thinking for yourself: create a few openings, see a gap in the market and move in. New services, new products. It's all about implementing new ideas, being flexible, ready to reorganise, diversify, restructure, being prepared to go where the smart money—'

'You're leaving Craigbar?'

That's not what he meant. A job, some cash, a crack at Alice Kerr – and he'd be a happy man.

'Nothing's settled yet. A few ideas, that's all.'

'Leaving the town? Not doing anything by halves are you, Steve? The school one day and Glasgow the next? Or Edinburgh? London? Sounds great. When are you off?'

He was about to shove Billy into the burn when he saw Alice Kerr coming along the path towards them. Her and Kirsty Thing. Immediately he started speaking louder.

'Like I was saying, Billy, I've plenty of ideas. Maybe start my own business.'

Alice Kerr was now only a few feet away.

And then even louder. 'There's a couple of good offers on the table, but I can't say more about them at present, you know how it is—'

A wave, a smile and she'd passed them by. Her and Kirsty Thing giggling to themselves.

Billy was asking him: 'Good offers – like what?'

'What?'

So much for Alice Kerr.

As usual, the telly was blasting away and the curtains were pulled shut at one side for a better picture. A programme about somewhere exotic with steel band music in the background.

When he came in, his father nodded to him, keeping his eyes on the screen, not looking so much bored as half-dead.

Steve took a deep breath. 'I'm leaving.'

Time passed. The steel band kept playing.

'I said, I'm leaving.'

His father zapped the TV into silence. 'I heard you the first time.' Then turned to face him. 'Running out on us, are you?'

'There's nothing much here.'

'And soon there'll be nothing minus you, that the idea?'

'But, Dad, there's nothing—'

'Streets paved with gold, eh? You mug!'

'But there's nothing here, Dad. You know that more than anyone. Years you've been laid off and—'

'You ungrateful wee shite!' His dad glared at him: 'I worked to keep us since before you were born, and now you're running out on us. No? Just when you might be bringing in something in return. Now the free board and lodging's over, you're off. Fucking years I worked—'

Steve switched off. He'd heard it all before.

When his dad zapped the sound back on, he left the room to the rhythms of a calypso.

His mother's coat lay on the kitchen table over a bag of shopping; she was going through her purse.

'Hello, Mum!'

She didn't look up. The purse was open in her hands and she seemed to be counting the small change.

'Mum?'

As he stood waiting for her to finish he could hear the calypso carrying on in the next room. It was getting dark outside. She'd not put on the light, and surely wouldn't be able to see properly what she was doing.

So he clicked on the switch by the door. That's when he realised she was crying. She'd heard everything through the wall.

The evening before he left, he went for a walk. A farewell tour of the town ending up in the Station Buffet for a few pints of Black Velvet with Billy.

Coming back across the railway bridge, he leant over for a last nostalgic glance at the wasteland beneath: heaps of broken bricks, grit, rubbish bags split open, a couple of upended cookers and a fridge lying on its side. When he was young, he'd played in the locomotive shed, the trains high above him in the half-light sweating burnt oil and diesel. He'd clambered off and on the footplates, pestering his dad and the other drivers for a ride. He'd been twelve when the shed was demolished, and a year later the rails had been pulled up. There was nothing to be seen now but a criss-cross of scars running in all directions.

He turned away and continued on home. He wasn't running out on anybody. If Craigbar was dying on its feet, he didn't intend to die with it. Simple as that. He'd hardly even started living.

3

Steve's Aunt Moira lived just outside Edinburgh, which was why he tried Dundee and Glasgow first. His mobile got nicked in Dundee – no great loss as it was nearly maxed out, and every time he switched it on he found it stacked with messages from his mother asking where he was and when was he going to his aunt's? He didn't fancy glooming it in Musselburgh, nor being told every ten minutes to wipe his shoes, mind the carpet, mind the woodwork, the surfaces, the sofa, to switch off the lights and leave the bathroom exactly as he found it. He'd usually ended up with somewhere to doss down – an empty bus in the Dundee bus station, the storeroom of a 24-hour garage where the guy took pity on him. No jobs though.

The following Sunday he got a lift in a fruit lorry and was no sooner in the warm cab than he fell fast asleep. Two hours later he woke to find himself hurtling south down the M74 – another hour and he'd be back in Craigbar. He baled out at the next turnoff.

The sign said 'Edinburgh, the Scenic Route'. Surely he could go to a big city like that without his aunt finding out. Once he'd got a flat and a job he could invite her round for afternoon tea, she'd like that.

It was a clear day as he walked into Moffat. He carried on the length of the main street and out again. His thumb held high and hopeful, he began the uphill march towards the Devil's Beef Tub.

Three hours later he was still marching. Did he look like a rapist, a robber, a terrorist? He tried to smile at the drivers, to look harmless, friendly. A complete waste of time. By late afternoon he'd come to a classic hitching-place: on a hill to make them go slower, no bends so he'd be clearly seen, and in front of a large lay-by where they could stop. No point in walking further. He took off his rucksack, he'd stay here still he turned into a skeleton – with its thumb out.

Time passed.

At last a car appeared. A Volvo with no passengers. Switch on his hopeful-but-getting-a-bit-dispirited look, thumb into overdrive. Maximum eye-contact, a cheery smile:

It blurred past at 70+. Fucker.

The silence afterwards felt as if the car's very speed had sucked all life out of the stretch of road where he was standing: no breath of wind remained, nothing but stone dykes, black tarmac, empty moorland and bare trees, clouds. He scuffed the loose gravel under his feet, then kicked a pebble to send it clattering against the dyke opposite:

'GOAAAAL!'

Out in this wilderness there was no crowd roaring from the stands, so he must be on telly with the sound down, a slow-motion action replay: pulling back his right foot, lining up for a rocket postage stamp in the top right-hand corner—

A lorry was hammering its way towards him on all cylinders.

Stepping back onto the grass verge, out with the thumb, on with the hopeful dispiritedness.

It was slowing down…for him or just because of the hill?

Move into full-pleading mode: handclasp in prayer.

It belches past.

Then stops. Twenty yards ahead; yes, you beauty! The lorry's stopped and stayed stopped with its engine running.

He picked up the rucksack and chased after it before the driver changed his mind.

The streetlights were coming on as they passed through Penicuik, the signpost said 'Edinburgh 12 miles'. Nearly there and getting nearer every minute. This was the life: sitting high in the cab with Radio 1 blasting away. The driver was called Dave.

'You'd be back there still, if I hadn't stopped. Drivers won't pick up nowadays. They're scared. Folk'll no hitch any more, they're scared as well. Everybody's getting more scared every day. You might be a desperate man for all I know, a terrorist.' Dave glanced over at him and they both laughed. 'Worst is – the wee hairies have gone as well. Give them a ride and they'd give you one back, just for the fun of it, for a good fry-up and to keep moving.' A half-smile. 'The wee hairies liked their drivers big and rugged!' Dave was a large man with a large laugh.

A furniture van was passing them. Dave flashed his lights to show when it was clear.

Maybe he could be a lorry-driver. He'd give Alice Kerr a lift. It would be a roasting hot day. She'd be wearing a really thin blouse, see-through almost—

'Are you on the run?'

Did he look like a criminal? A hard man? 'From the cops, you mean? No. I'm going to Edinburgh to get myself a job.'

'Take my advice, son, and get the hell out of this country while you're young. Scotland's a midden, and the south's worse. Gridlock from Birmingham on down. New Labour's just New Tory, America was once a colony of ours – now we're just one of theirs, and dragged in to fight their wars. Get yourself to Canada, Australia, anywhere.' He grinned. 'End of sermon.'

It was getting dark now and starting to rain. The *swish-swish* of the wipers, and he was in danger of dozing off: Alice Kerr was getting into his cab; she was smiling, her short skirt sliding up—

'Somewhere to stay, have you?'

'I've been there lots of times before – plenty of places. No problem. My aunt's in Musselburgh if I don't find anything.'

'I'll give you an address before I drop you: Giorgio's, he's Italian. It's no Hilton, mind, but was cheap enough and clean enough last time I was there. A place to start from, he does food as well. Keep you out a cardboard box for one night anyway.'

They had reached the outskirts of Edinburgh now and were passing a large factory. He could see the rain hammering down into puddles under the security lights. Soon he'd have to leave the warm cab.

By the time Dave dropped him, the rain had stopped. He walked down Lothian Road – lights blazing on both sides, the street traffic-jammed, the pavements heaving with ravers, bars everywhere, restaurants, clubs, the lot. This time on a Sunday night Craigbar was quieter than the dark side of the moon, but here was real action. Techno boomed out of a pub as he went past, the women looked dressed up for the kind of parties he'd only read about. He'd go down to Princes Street first, to check out the action. Then something to eat, a place to stay. He'd arrived.

Half an hour later, with his back against one of its stone pillars, he was sitting on the steps of the RSA Gallery: the castle on one side, the big shops on the other. City bustle all round him. He'd nearly forty quid left and no one to tell him what to do. The city was his. This time tomorrow he'd have a job, maybe in that Virgin megastore he'd passed, or in one of the clubs in Lothian Road. Somewhere cool anyway. And a bedsit or, better still, a room in a flat like in *Friends* – one that had parties every weekend.

On a step further along a woman sat mumbling to herself like someone praying; she had two coats on. Suddenly she slapped herself on the cheek. Then another slap. A moment later her lips moved and the prayer continued. A daftie. His bum was getting cold on the stone; he'd move soon.

With his head leaning back against the pillar he could hear the taxis belting down the Mound; some pigeons were arguing over by the railings; a ghetto-blaster went past punching it out. He could hear the city, he could *feel* it – Craigbar was fucking nowhere.

Someone had just sat down not far from him. He could smell them. He opened his eyes and saw a man with a blotchy red face, a tangled red beard and red hair.

'Bastards!' The tramp was shouting at nobody: 'Paid my share and drunk my share, no more and no less.' Real Glasgow accent. 'Fucking Highlanders: don't drink with them, son. They'd have the sugar out your tea, not that any of them has seen tea in a long time. Fucking Highlanders!'

A headbanger. He looked about thirty. He was filthy and pissed. Seriously pissed.

'I'll have my wee smoke here in peace, eh no?' He took a few dog-ends apart, rolling them into one cigarette. He was swaying backwards and forwards with the effort. 'Sorry there's not enough to go round.'

'Don't smoke, thanks.' Not that he would have smoked that turdy-looking fag anyway.

'Scottish too! Some fucking country, eh? But I've travelled, let me tell you. Fucking Gulf, fucking desert – the whole fucking trip.' The tramp prodded the last of the tobacco in with a match. His cigarette lit, the paper flared up at the end and went out. 'A fucking country this and a half-fucking country that.' He shook his fist.

A mega-headbanger. The man tried to get to his feet, fell heavily back onto the steps and slumped over to one side, the cigarette still between his fingers.

Time to move. Steve stood up, shouldered his rucksack and started along Princes Street. He was starving. In for a quick Burger King. Out again. He was sure to get a job next day so he could stretch to a cheap B&B. A shower, recycle the underwear and socks, then head out for a night on the town.

Should he look for Giorgio's? The address said 'along the Cowgate', which didn't sound too promising. In a city this big there'd be plenty other places.

An hour later he found himself back on Lothian Road. Almost half past nine by the clock at Tollcross. No point in going down to the city centre again so he took a different street, slightly uphill, past office buildings that were all glass. Then past an old Victorian-looking pile: 'Former Edinburgh Royal Infirmary – Luxury Apartments Development'. Just like in Craigbar. He was suddenly very tired.

By ten-thirty he'd tried several B&B's that were either too expensive, or full, mostly both. A few others wouldn't answer the door. He was getting nowhere and his rucksack was getting heavier. The main streets were useless, nothing but shops, so he turned into a side street and walked a few yards.

'What the fuck are you staring at?' A man's voice from the doorway in front of him.

'Nothing, nobody.' He'd not been staring, just looking at the tangle of dirty blankets lying on a sheet of plastic; the doorway was set back from the street.

'This is my doss.' The man was getting to his feet.

'I wasn't staring. Honest.' He turned to go back to the main street.

'Hey! Wait!'

He should keep going, but the dosser was right behind him.

'Where are you going?'

'Just off. Nowhere. Doesn't matter.' Was he going to get beaten up? The man looked quite small and not very tough, thank fuck.

'Looking for a doss, are you? A place to kip?' Not threatening any more, not even angry.

Steve shrugged. 'A bed, or something.'

'You've missed the shelters. Either the Sheraton now, or the street…and it'll not be the Sheraton, I'm thinking.'

'No, not tonight.'

'Look, you know what it's like round here: two's safer than one. You can doss back there with me.'

'How d'you mean, "safer"?'

'There's crazies round here, man. Wandering around all night. I thought you were one of them. They hate people. Out of their fucking heads. Two's safer. Come on.'

'I don't know. A bed would—'

'There's no fucking beds, I'm telling you. You been in the city long?'

'Mmm…a few hours.'

'Fuck's sake! You need looking after, walking around here at night. Come on, you'll be safer. We both will. If anyone does come, there'll be the two of us. Sleeping-bag?'

'Yes.'

'Good. I'm Harry. You're not gay, are you?'

A few minutes later he was in his bag, stretched out on the plastic sheeting and a piece of blanket. 'The real cold comes from under,' Harry had told him. He was wearing all his clothes and had his rucksack for a pillow; because the blanket smelt rancid, he'd laid his scarf up next to his face. From time to time there were shouts from further down the street; whenever anyone went past, he opened his eyes, held his breath. The ground seemed to get colder and colder, and harder. His first night in Edinburgh – things could only improve.

4

Someone was kicking his feet. He was cold. Rigid with cold – cold that had seeped right to the marrow of his bones, and frozen solid. The kicking got harder.

Crazies? He opened his eyes. A red-faced, elderly woman stood glaring down at him. No sign of Harry. Just his blanket and plastic sheet.

'I said OUT! Or I'm calling the police. It's not a hotel here, is it?'

'Okay, missus.' He was so cold he almost creaked as he sat up.

'It's bloody well not okay, is it? My shop this is, not a doss-house. Get moving.'

'I'm going. Don't fash yourself.'

'Don't what myself? You – you vermin! The police it is.'

Out of his sleeping-bag, his rucksack shouldered, and he was belting down the street in seconds. He caught sight of himself as he passed a large supermarket window and laughed: if only Dave the driver could see him now – he was on the run right enough.

Half an hour later. A café. Some people staring at newspapers, the rest staring at nothing; the windows were steamed over and condensation was running down the glass. A cup of tea and two bacon rolls (£37.70 left). Now for his paper: a job first, or a flat? 'Accommodation Wanted' was three times longer than 'Accommodation To Let', where there was nothing under £50 per week. So, even if he found £10 in the street, walked all the way there, and the room was still free, and they took him in at a reduced rate, he'd still not be able to eat until he got paid at the end of the week for a job he'd not even started looking for yet. So, fuck that – he'd try for a job first. A bite out of the second roll, folding the paper to read the 'Vacancies' top left: packers, cleaners, barmen, messengers. Plenty of jobs.

He ringed a few, finished his breakfast, had a wash and smarten-up in the café toilet before leaving to find a phone box. Once he'd got a job there'd be no more dead-end cafés for him: he'd soon have a place of his own, a sound system to keep things sweet, and raves every weekend where he'd meet one of the eager-looking girls he'd seen on Lothian Road. They'd looked eager enough for anything, even him.

Six hours' phoning and going to places. Result – fuck-all. Either the job was taken or he was too young or he was told to leave his name and address...HA-HA-FUCKING-HA! He wasted a fortune on phone calls and fares, especially one out to Bathgate for a job that they filled just as he was on his way there. They'd told him to come, too. Must have told everyone, the fuckers.

It was raining again. Lunch had been a pie and cup of polystyrene coffee in a bus shelter. That was hours ago, so he went into a McDonald's at the beginning of Princes Street (£26.15 left). Another glance down the job columns. The paper was sodden, most of the adverts now crossed out, and ripped where he'd put his pen through the Bathgate ad. A few were still circled: no reply or only answer machines. Maybe he should be trying to find a B&B for tonight, or looking for Giorgio's. Either that or it'd be another doorway, and this time he'd be by himself if the crazies came. The cheapest B&B in the paper was a backpackers' hostel at £12 a night. Meaning: two nights, then Cardboard City, or else his Aunt Moira's.

Dinner over. A whole day's tramping around with fuck-all to show for it but sore feet. It would be getting dark soon. A megabar of chocolate (£25.05 left). His rucksack was cutting into him; he was freezing cold and sweating at the same time. By now his mum and dad would have had their tea and be settling themselves down for an evening of telly in front of a warm fire – he, meanwhile, was standing on a traffic island at the east end of Princes Street in the pissing rain.

A bus dieselled him in the face as it swung round towards North Bridge. Opposite was the Balmoral Hotel: storey upon storey of thick pile carpets, limitless hot water, meals, maids and beds; at the front door a man in a kilt was greeting a couple of Japanese suits and their wives whose luggage was being carried in for them by kilt number two. Lucky them.

The green man. He should cross.

But why bother? He wasn't going to the Balmoral. He wasn't going up North Bridge either, or along Princes Street. He wasn't going anywhere.

He turned and went back on to the pavement he'd left a red man ago. Ahead of him, away from Princes Street, was the hill with that Greek temple on top. Calton Hill it was called, one of the tourist sights. He might as well go and have a look, then at least he'd have done something. And afterwards? He shrugged: when you're going nowhere – what's the rush?

Ten minutes sweatier and colder, he was standing on Calton Hill. Big deal. A lumpy stretch of grass with Greek-looking pillars stuck in it. But at least the rain had stopped and the view was good: the whole city spread out in the growing darkness. More and more lights coming on. The Castle, Walter Scott Monument, Princes Street, the RSA Gallery – if he'd come up here at the start he'd have seen the whole lot in one fucking go and saved on the feet. Maybe he should head straight for the bus station, he could be in Musselburgh and his Aunt Moira's in less than an hour.

'Bright lights, big city?' A small guy in a leather coat was standing beside him. Where had he come from?

'Aye, they're bright.' Maybe he really should go to his Aunt Moira's?

'You're not from Edinburgh, are you?' Moustache, going bald, creepy-looking smile.

'No.' At least his Aunt Moira's would be warm and he could have a bath, a proper meal.

'A lovely Borders accent you've got. In fact, to tell you a little secret…' the man moved a step nearer and lowered his voice almost to a whisper, 'I'd noticed you even before I heard you speak.'

'Yeah?' Aunt Moira's it was. A base. Soon as he got a job he could move out.

'I noticed you as I was passing and thought to myself, now *there's* someone.'

How many fucking headbangers were there in this city, and what was this one after? His money? His bum? Or what?

Time to go.

'A nice boy, not like the others round here. Dirt. Filth.' A look of disgust directed into the darkness that was beginning to surround them both. 'And all the time you turn out to be from the Borders, a pure country boy, which proves it.' Again the creepy smile, and he seemed to be standing much nearer than before. 'A little drink to celebrate? Not far from here. Shall we?'

The creep touched him on the arm.

'No way.' Steve took a step back.

'Not far. A drink and a chat. No funny business, nothing like that. Just the two of us.' The creep's hand was touching him again.

'No way, I said. Just leave me alone, will you.' He turned to walk off.

The creep was right beside him. 'No funny business, I promise.'

He kept on down the hill towards Princes Street.

The creep was still with him.

He walked faster. 'Fuck off, will you. Just FUCK OFF!'

'Nasty little boy, eh?'

Suddenly there were two creeps, one on each side of him. Creep number two was much bigger.

'Nasty little boy you've got here. Needs taught a lesson.'

Creep number two was also wearing a leather coat, but his

moustache looked stuck on. Like he was a joke – only he wasn't. No way.

'They're just not strict enough in schools these days.'

One of them gripped his arm. He pulled himself free and ran.

And kept running. Clattered down the stone steps. Dodged in and out between pedestrians. The two creeps pounding after him.

He ran faster, keeping on downhill for speed. Pushing past people. A gap in the traffic. The screech of a taxi braking, but he didn't stop. Into a side street, up another side street. Back onto the main road.

Once he was sure they'd given up, he slowed to walking pace; he was sweating, drenched through, and his rucksack weighed a ton. Where the hell was he? These guys would have been seriously bad news if they'd caught him. From now on he wouldn't speak to anyone – and no more doorways, no headbangers, no creeps...

It made sense to go to his aunt's...but it felt like he was just giving in, especially after getting chased by those two weirdo-creeps. Anyway, he'd dealt with them – he'd survived.

He straightened his back and began marching back up Leith Walk towards the city centre. It was too soon for Aunt Moira's. He'd try Giorgio's first.

With detours and wrong directions it took him nearly an hour to reach the Cowgate and a badly lit close: opposite was a wasteground of litter and a half-demolished building, this side was a line of blackened tenements. Giorgio's was supposed to be nearby.

It was well after ten when he saw the battered sign *Café and Accommodation*. Because the window had been partly painted over he couldn't get a good look in, but a light was on. It certainly looked cheap. At least he'd be able to take off his rucksack for a few minutes.

The place was cramped with unmatched plastic tables jammed

together; floorboards showed through ancient-looking green lino. Three men were sitting at separate tables; they glanced at him and said nothing. They had the same 'mugged' look as his dad, but worse. Real deadbeats. One of them was holding a newspaper, the other two were just sitting. Behind the counter a plump man swivelled himself round on a stool; his face had a greasy shine, a thin tidemark of hair was smeared across his scalp.

'Yes?' A foreign accent. He must be Giorgio.

'A cup of tea, please. And do you do food?'

'Only snacks left: slice of bread – 15p butter; 10p marge. Hamburger £1.'

Steve wished he'd gone for another McDonald's instead. 'Hamburger, please, and a tea.'

Should he mention lorry-driver Dave? Maybe then the man would be a bit friendlier.

Giorgio had already swivelled himself back round to start frying a piece of sliced sausage in a pan of what smelt like diesel oil. Just as well he was very hungry.

'Onions?' Giorgio's back did the talking. '15p extra.'

Why not live a little? 'Aye, some onions.'

He stood. He waited. He starved.

At last Giorgio swivelled back round. '£1.65.'

He carried his cup and plate over to an empty table next to the wall where he ate his way through what tasted like a roll of burnt onion with a slice of burnt lard in the middle (£23.40 left). The tea was hot and wet. He was starving and so…another round of tea and lard.

Without speaking Giorgio served him and took his money. He sat and ate. No one looked at him. No one spoke. On the wall opposite was a poster advertising Sicily: a beach with white sand where it was a beautiful summer's day of blue sky and blue sea. Part of the sky and cliff in the top left corner was torn and had been sellotaped.

Two hard-looking guys came through a doorway at the back of the café.

'Be good boys now,' Giorgio called after them. Once they'd gone out into the street, he added, 'Better when they go.' He put two chalk marks on a board behind him before swivelling back to sit facing the café again, his hands resting on his paunch.

'In *this* country...' The deadbeat reading glanced up from his paper, 'in this country, I say, a man is innocent until proved guilty.' He glared at everyone. 'Am I right?'

'Innocent?' Giorgio wiped the counter with a dirty dishcloth. 'They innocent? Then I not born.' He continued washing cups in a small sink.

More minutes passed.

Now for the room. Picking up his rucksack, Steve approached the counter.

Giorgio's back asked him: 'More tea?'

'No, thank you. Do you have any rooms?'

Giorgio let the cup he was washing slide back into the greasy water, and swivelled round.

'Is bed you want?'

'Yes. How much is a bed?'

The man looked at him closely. 'Is late. How much you got? You DHSS?'

'No.'

'Better DHSS.' Giogio shrugged. 'You want bed. I show you.' He stepped down from his stool, came out from behind his counter and waddled plumply towards the doorway at the back of the café. 'You come.' He was wearing slippers.

They went upstairs and along an uncarpeted corridor to a door with a bare light bulb hanging above it.

'Here.'

The room was large, crowded, and smelt worse than the school gym. A dozen or so bunk-beds were crammed along the walls, both windows were shut and had beds in front of them. Even with the light on, some people seemed to be asleep. In the centre a man of about sixty was standing pot-bellied in his underwear, pulling on his trousers; at a small washhand basin in the corner another was shaving.

'Your bed here.' Giorgio pointed to a lower bunk. 'This for your stuff.' A black plastic bin-bag was taped to the side. 'You pay, I bring sheets. Clean sheets.'

The pillow had several grey hairs lying on it, and several red ones.

Cleanliness-wise things must have gone downhill since Dave the driver's last visit. Giorgio was looking closely at him. '£10 this night. You want?'

'Well, I'll have to see. It depends.'

'You see now. You pay now.' He prodded the mattress. 'Good bed. You want? You not want?'

An old man with no teeth gazed down at him from the top bunk, then grinned, nodded his head and gave him the thumbs-up. Another daftie?

'Is late – make special price: £8. I busy man. I get sheets. Come.'

Out of the smell at least, back along the corridor, down the stairs.

The same three deadbeats were sitting exactly as before.

In the corner was a large cupboard. 'Sheets here.' Giorgio had just unlocked it when the telephone started to ring. The cupboard door was locked again. 'You wait.'

Giorgio returned behind his counter, heaved himself up onto his swivel chair and took the phone.

Steve remained where he was. As there was nothing much else in the room he pretended to be interested in the poster of Sicily. Behind the counter Giorgio was swivelling himself from side to side in irritation as he half-scolded half-pleaded, it seemed, in Italian with whoever was at the other end.

After a few minutes' awkwardly standing around in the middle of the room, Steve moved to a nearby table and sat down.

Wouldn't he be better off at his Aunt Moira's? Or back home? Back at school even? Once more he glanced over at the poster of the beach in Sicily. Why did Giorgio want to live in a dump like this when he could be in a country of sun and blue skies and the Mediterranean? The three deadbeats looked as if they'd been in the room, sitting at their separate tables, all their lives. Was he going to be deadbeat number four?

Suddenly he was aware that the man at the next table had just said something out loud, maybe even to him.

'Sorry?'

The man laid down his newspaper and leant across. 'I said, it's always the first few days are the worst.'

The first few days of what? Over by the counter, the murmur of Giorgio's scolding and pleading rose and fell while the rest of the room sat in silence.

'And after the first few days?' asked Steve. 'What then?'

The man shrugged and went back to his paper.

Next morning he was out of Giorgio's within minutes of waking up. While he sat in McDonald's finishing the last of his McBreakfast or whatever it was called (£11.80 left), he had a quick glance at the tattered remains of yesterday's paper. There was one advert he'd not tried phoning yet. He had no experience, he was probably too young – it would be a waste of thirty pence. But if things did work out, the job would be the answer to his problems, to all of them at once. And if they didn't? Worst-case scenario was a few nights at Aunt Moira's, which, compared to Giorgio's shit-hole or dossing on the streets, suddenly seemed almost attractive.

Five minutes later Steve went to the toilets to give himself the full 100,000-mile service. Off with the T-shirt, some hard-core scrubbing, rubbing and scraping. Brush the teeth, the hair. Then on with his cleanest shirt, a jersey to cover the creases. He should look reliable, neat, pleasant, honest, serious, trustworthy, hardworking – and servile. A quick practice in the mirror trying out different facial expressions for each. Final thumbs-up and he was ready to go.

His interview was at noon. He arrived quarter of an hour early. *Posh* he'd expected, but not quite *this* posh: a massive three-storey townhouse in Heriot Row, with its own railings and a flight of stone steps down to the basement. Time for a quick stroll up and down the street, a peer into the centre of the square – into the locked private gardens with their trees, neat paths, bushes and well-cut lawns. Then back to the house. Up the front steps, lift the brass knocker and…*knock-knock*.

Afterwards he was told he'd been favourably considered precisely *because* he had no experience. Having no bad habits – Billy'd get a laugh out of that, he thought – he could then be trained from the beginning. He could be *moulded*. The important thing was that he seemed polite, and he stood well. He would rarely be expected to speak. The wage was not large, but if he did his work properly there would be substantial tips.

That evening he phoned home.

His mum started in immediately: Where was he? Why hadn't he phoned? Hadn't he got her messages? She'd been almost out of her mind with worry. When he explained about his mobile getting stolen she calmed down for a moment and asked if he was all right. He was fine, he said. Couldn't be better. He was in Edinburgh and—

What about his Aunt Moira?

'Well, I…'

His Aunt Moira had been half-expecting him all week, had he at least let *her* know what he was up to?

Steve put in another twenty pence. 'I've got a job, Mum.'

After a well-judged pause for dramatic effect, he announced that the job couldn't be better, that it was perfect. It came with a place to stay and full board and full training – and he'd already started.

There was a long silence, until he realised his mum had burst into tears.

Then his dad took over – a rant about upsetting his mother, then another about the cost of phoning mobiles, even just to leave a message. His dad's third rant – his disgust at hearing that his own son had become 'a lackey of capitalism' – got cut off when the money ran out.

That was that over with. He'd phone Billy tomorrow.

Getting to sleep was difficult that night. Not just because it was a new house, a new bed and that a church clock somewhere nearby chimed the half-hour…No, it was because he couldn't stop thinking about the cocktail parties and dinner parties to come, the business conferences and receptions, the women. Most of all, the women…

5

It was 8.30 a.m. His recent travels aside, since retiring from Craigbar High School he'd expected to be still in bed this time on a weekday morning, getting himself three-legged thinking about Alice Kerr. Instead, here he was in a room with closed curtains and all the lights blazing, standing in front of a full-length mirror and being dressed by a real butler. Over on the bedside table someone was being interviewed on the radio about Baghdad and Falluja. Back in Nowhere-Land his dad would be getting himself psyched up for another day of *This Morning*, *Des and Mel*, *Richard and Judy*, *Neighbours*, *Hollyoaks*; Billy'd be sweating over another history project...

'Ow! That hurt, Francis.'

'Try to keep still, please, Steve. We're almost finished.' A final press on the new footman's offending collar stud and the butler stood back to admire the effect. 'Excellent, Steve. Now remember, a good footman is discreet, he is silent unless spoken to. He is invisible.'

Steve nodded.

They'd been at it for nearly half an hour so far. Starched shirt − like wearing a piece of cornflakes packet − wing collar, bow-tie, striped waistcoat, razor-creased trousers, cufflinks, studs and black jacket with state-of-the-art tails. Was that really him there in the mirror? Steve Merrick, ex-environmental student and doorway dosser? He nodded at his reflection, and the footman in full livery nodded back.

'Right, Steve. A final twirl.'

Round he went. Billy would've pissed himself.

Steve spent the rest of the day learning how to get dressed by himself, how to stand correctly, how to walk, hold a tray (for drinks, for canapés and at dinner), how to set a table, lay out cutlery (first course on the outside, knife blade always facing inwards), which glasses were meant for which wines, how to lay out clothes, how to press or iron clothes for immediate wear, how to hang and pack clothes for travelling, which were the appropriate clothes for the appropriate time of day, how to address a duke, a lord, an earl, an ambassador (and their ladies), how to address other staff. He was a busy young footman.

Time: evening of the following day, 6.30 p.m.

Place: the hallway of a 3-storey, Georgian townhouse in the

Grange. Enter Steve Merrick, the perfect footman from top to toe:

—Haircut

—Shave

—Wing collar and bow-tie

—Starched white shirt

—Striped waistcoat

—Black swallowtail jacket

—Pressed trousers seamed with black piping

—Mirror-polished black shoes

The problem was, dressed like this he didn't look the least bit invisible. Anything but.

Steve was doing the door-and-coats: Open the door, and bow / Open the door, and bow.

Good evening, sir/Good evening, madam.

Your coat, sir?/Your coat, madam?

The men wore dinner-jackets; the women evening frocks and perfume. No one acted surprised at being greeted by a liveried footman – their nod of acknowledgement was followed each time by a glance that treated him as invisible, thus allowing the door to open and close of its own accord, it seemed, and the coats to be whisked from sight as if by magic. Later, when he served in the main reception room, his invisibility made dishes of canapés appear out of nowhere, wine glasses fill themselves.

The first awkward moment came when a drunk touched him on the arm, nearly upsetting his drinks tray. 'You look just like a Christmas parcel tied up in a bow,' was whispered in his ear. Steve ignored him.

Then it was back to the door-and-coats. A few minutes after he'd returned to his post in the hall a second drunk stumbled through from the reception room.

At once Steve moved into strict footman-mode: rigid-straight stance, eyes front. A statue. The drunk, mid-thirties, balding, zigzagged towards him. Then stared at him. Then staggered round him. Finally there was a nod as if the footman had passed inspection. Close to, Steve could see the sweat-sheen on the man's face, and smell his wine-breath. Pissed.

Footman-voice: 'Your coat, sir?'

Wine-breath's eyes were sliding all over the place. Seriously pissed.

Public-school voice. 'Greetings, white man.'

'Would you like your coat, sir?'

Wine-breath took a clumsy step backwards. 'Why – why?'

For the third time: 'Would you like your coat, sir?'

'A servant, so why aren't you a different colour? Why?' The eyes slipped away to one side, then returned. 'Or are you deaf as well?'

No coat wanted – Steve would say nothing.

'Trying to help you. Understand?'

The man looked like Billy usually looked just before throwing up. A discreet footman-step out of range.

'Lose you your job if I wanted. Just like that.' Wine-breath clicked his fingers in his face. 'Understand?'

Footman-silence.

'If you were black or brown, it wouldn't matter.' He began weaving up and down the hall. 'Wouldn't even notice you, black or brown.' The bammer came to an abrupt stop and stared at him. 'Opening the door for us, handing us our coats. People treating you like dirt.' He began pacing again. 'Black or brown, people wouldn't think you were dirt doing a dirt job, because you'd be black or brown. Understand?' Another stare. 'But white and doing a dirt job, people think you're dirt…Don't keep backing away from me.' Wine-breath came close to him again. 'You and I,' he tapped Steve on the chest, 'we're on the sane side, the *same* side I mean. And this time we're prepared.' He reached into his pocket.

Only a cigarette-case.

Wine-breath tried to fumble it open, let it fall, then stood swaying. 'Dropped my cigarette-case.'

Was he expected to pick it up? Why couldn't the bammer fuck off and annoy someone else?

'No.' Wine-breath made to push him away though Steve hadn't even moved. 'Stay there, you're not *my* servant. You and me, white man, we're on the same side. Remember?'

It was taking the drunk forever to reach down. Getting upright again, he staggered backwards till he collided with the wall. He leant against it, then tried standing up straight again.

'Barbarians now, even the white ones. Filling the streets. Night, you can't tell them from the rubbish.' He opened the case and gazed into it for several seconds. It was empty. He put it back in his pocket. 'All chaos now. All gone to pot. If you're black or brown or a Jew or a Muslim or gay even, you know who you are and who to stand on, know your standing, I mean – but the rest of us…'

'Ah, there you are, Brodie, we thought we'd lost you.'

Steve turned to see a woman coming through from the party, the front of her black dress teasing her breasts up until they seemed almost within reach. He felt her glance pass over him as over the other furniture in the hall.

'Needed to be alone, did you?' She waved her empty glass in the direction of the main room. 'Feeling a bit tired? All that chat-chat, nice-nice…so exhausting, don't you think? You need reviving. Kiss of Life?' She went up to Brodie, pursing her lips and making soft kissing sounds while sliding her hands over her hips. 'Or something a little stronger?'

Steve felt himself getting hard.

Her empty glass was shoved in his direction. 'Fill that.'

He took her glass and looked on while she put her arms around wine-breath's neck and pressed herself against him.

'Come on, Brodie.' A very sexy laugh. 'Mary'll have a room off here. Come on.'

Fuck, he was getting more rigid by the moment. No way was he fetching champagne for her, not with his stiffie going into the reception room first and him following.

Wine-breath was trying to free himself when, with an abrupt movement, she released him.

'Not up to it?' Then the slightest nod of her head towards Steve: 'This one would in a moment.'

Steve clasped the glass in front of him, and held on.

'They hardly ever get it; he's been staring at me ever since I came in. Not like you. Take me for granted you do. Always.' She began pretend-sobbing about how she wasn't loved and was always taken for granted. Less than a minute later the two of them returned to the party.

Steve put down her glass on a hall table and tried not to think about her breasts, her tight dress, the tone of her voice saying, 'This one would in a moment.' Too right he would: in one of the side rooms, on the floor, against the wall, anywhere...

An elderly couple came through from the reception room. He had to get himself unstiffed.

Coat, sir? Coat, madam?/Goodbye, sir./Goodbye, madam.

And off they went out the door. The whole party in reverse order until there were only two coats left, and then none.

Francis brought him a glass of champagne. Then he drank three glasses of orange juice and another champagne. Jackets off, and everyone began clearing away the debris of paper napkins, plates, glasses, bottles and tablecloths smeared with dip. The faster they worked the quicker they could leave. Lastly the rubbish was put into bin-bags and packed into the van. The furniture was returned to the room and everything was once again exactly as when they had arrived.

Come early Friday afternoon he was in the circular dining-room hard at work, as usual. Today he was practising different ways to fold linen napkins: having done a dozen mitres he was now onto lilies. Halfway through another sex-free day in Scotland's capital city, he was not one grope closer to losing his virginity than he'd been back in Craigbar. Not that he'd ever had much hopes of Alice Kerr or even Kirsty Thing. But someone. Anyone. His lunchtime stroll along George Street had been torture. Office workers and shop assistants, women and girls. Wherever he looked: cleavages, bare midriffs, short skirts...

Just then, Francis dashed in through the door:

'We've had an emergency call for staff at a country-house do. Their part-timer can't make it. A footman for a house party. How do you feel about going there alone? I know it's a lot to ask as you've only just started, Steve, but the butler there will keep you right. Mr Todd. He's a stickler, old-style. But fair...more or less.'

'Fine.'

Francis handed him a piece of paper. 'Good man! Here's where you're going. Train's in forty minutes – you'll have to rush.'

Steve looked at the address. Then looked again.

6

Craigbar House was a mega-mansion not much smaller than the main building of Steve's former school. It was older and in much better shape, the front lawn could have contained the school playing fields twice over. The on-expenses taxi swept straight past the grand-looking, pillar-and-portico front entrance and took Steve round to the back of the house. It dropped him, and the suitcase Francis had lent him, at the kitchen door. The servants' entrance. The driver just seemed to know.

Fare paid and receipt in his pocket, Steve got out and rang the bell. The taxi turned a full circle in the courtyard, then drove off. Steve rang again. And again. And waited.

Craigbar House, for fuck's sake – a twenty-minute walk down the main road and he could join Billy and the rest of them chilling out in Franco's café. Alice Kerr and Kirsty Thing might even be there. His mum would soon be getting in from work, his dad'd be slobbing himself through the last hour of daytime television.

Steve rang again, this time keeping his finger on the bell. He glanced round at the courtyard, the stables opposite, the wintry-looking tennis court, the stripped woods. A house this big, there had to be someone who'd answer...

Abruptly he lifted his finger from the bell.

The glower from a pair of seventy-year-old, steel-wool eyebrows filled the doorway. They were not amused. Below them were a scowl, a black suit, black tie and matching black shoes. This had to be the butler.

'Hello, Mr Todd, I'm Steve Merrick.'

The eyebrows glared at him in silence. They were taking aim.

'The footman for the house party. From the agency.'

The eyebrows fired. 'You're late. The guests will be here soon. Follow me.' The butler marched off along the corridor and disappeared round the corner.

Steve picked up his suitcase and hurried after. Not a good start.

Down a dark passage, past a kitchen where two women were clattering pots and pans, and chatting – they didn't turn to look at him. A radio was playing, a food mixer whirred. Mr Todd had already reached the end of the second corridor and was about to vanish again. Steve hurried faster. Then came a stone staircase, another corridor, another staircase getting narrower and stonier and darker the higher they went. Another staircase. The suitcase banged against his leg every few steps, but the butler didn't slow down or even glance back at him.

Finally Mr Todd came to a stop. Steve almost ran right into him. The butler threw open the door.

'Your room. Downstairs in fifteen minutes. Butler's pantry's beyond the kitchen. Follow the servants' corridor, keep off the carpets and you'll find it easy enough, I'm sure, a smart boy like you.'

The room seemed larger once Mr Todd had gone. The butler didn't like him, probably he didn't like anyone. A bed, an armchair, a chest of drawers all to himself; a door in the corner of the room led to a private en-suite bathroom. A book, *Scottish Clans*, lay on the bedside table. Stamped on the inside cover were the words: *This book has been removed from a bedroom in Craigbar House*. Some chance.

Quickest of quick showers in his private bathroom, then the once-over in the mirror: winged, studded, cuffed, bow-tied and tailed. Three minutes left to find Mr Todd's pantry.

Out the door, then turn right. Along the corridor and through the door at the end. No good, carpeted, this part was for guests, not for servants. Once he found the stone stairs and kept going down he'd reach the pantry, eventually.

More corridors, more doors, more stone stairs, until at last he heard a radio up ahead. Cooking smells. The kitchen, he must be nearly there. Maybe worth slowing down for a moment to check out the talent? One of the women he'd seen when he arrived was stacking plates on a tray. She turned.

There was a moment's pause.

'Steve Merrick!'

'Alice Kerr! Hello, I—'

'This way, Merrick.' Mr Todd was suddenly beside him.

'I – I was just coming.'

As he hurried after the butler he heard Alice laughing.

The butler's pantry lay between the kitchen and the dining-room. Everything was very compact, like being on board ship. The cupboards, the shelves, the table, the floor and even the sink itself with its sliding cover, were made of wood.

Alice Kerr.

'They were Napoleon's.' Mr Todd pointed to some glasses standing on the draining board. 'That's his crest.'

Alice Kerr. Alice Kerr.

There was an ornate *NB* worked on each glass. The man who had conquered all of Europe had actually touched them, a few of them at least, assuming he hadn't done his own washing-up.

'So when you go to pick them up. Don't. *I* look after the Napoleon glasses.'

Alice Kerr.

Under the butler's direction Steve brought two trayloads of cutlery from the pantry and helped lay the table. There were to be six at dinner: two guests on either side, the host and hostess at the ends. The shiny surface was checked from every angle for dust marks, fingerprints, polish residue. The centrepiece was a black ebony elephant glittering with precious stones. The knives and forks were solid gold, the heavy linen napkins folded neatly. A trayload of glasses came next, there was to be a nest of three wine glasses at each place.

Mr Todd muttered loudly. 'Save time if we just gave them three bottles each.'

Finally the job was finished. It had taken well over half an hour. Steve was then shown a brass stud fixed into the floor next to the host's chair. When Mr Todd pressed on it with his foot, they heard a bell ring through in the pantry. With the door closed, the diners would notice nothing.

'As soon as Mr Grant-Jamieson rings, you come through and clear away the plates whether or not the other guests have finished. That is most important, his specific instructions. Remember: the bell: come through at once: remove the plates. Is that clear? Mr Grant-Jamieson does not expect to be kept waiting.'

Steve nodded.

The butler gave the table a last inspection, then, having corrected the alignment of one of the glasses, he stood up very straight, turned to face the door and walked off. His voice came back from along the corridor. 'Follow me, Merrick.'

The main hall was straight out of a horror movie: marble floor, garage-sized fireplace, a stamp-album wall of stags' heads, antlers and family portraits. As they walked across the open space to the foot of the stairs their footsteps echoed around them. Hung straight in front and above, where the central staircase divided into two, was a cinema-screen-sized oil painting of tangled arms, legs, weapons, horses, cannons, torn flags, dirt and varnish.

The butler called to him from halfway up the stairs:

'Come along...but don't run.' Todd's voice boomed and echoed in the emptiness. 'Doubtless in the city everyone runs, but not here.'

They set off along the corridor until they came to two doors facing each other. Mr Todd entered the one on the right.

'The Mandalay Room.'

The old-fashioned bed was the only solid thing in the room – the rest was a clutter of rickety-looking bamboo cabinets, chairs and a table, all of which looked like so much misplaced garden furniture. A painting hung above the fireplace – a mountain landscape that was mostly mist, with a temple, a lake, and oriental writing scrolling down from some clouds. The lampshade had bits of thread and glass balls dangling from it. Like an upmarket Chinese carry-out place.

'Mr Grant-Jamieson's grandfather governed a territory larger than the whole of Scotland.' A pause for him to be impressed, then: 'Mr Wallingham, the noted financier, will occupy this room. Mr Cavendish – a man of great influence with the new Scottish Parliament – will be in the Bangalore Room opposite. Follow me.'

Another carry-out place, Indian this time, with masks and

rugs on the walls together with framed photographs showing a veranda crammed with dark servants gathered around a white family. A tiger-skin rug lay in front of the fireplace, a hollowed-out elephant's foot held the poker and fire-tongs. Mr Todd indicated a wriggly-carved doorway in the corner of the room.

'The gentleman's bathroom is through there.'

Then the window. 'The curtains, of course, are electric.'

'Hmm.'

The steel-wool eyebrows glared at him. Was he supposed to say, Hmm, *sir*?

The butler pressed a switch to check the curtains were running smoothly.

'Have you given service at many house parties?'

'This is my first.'

The curtains stopped in mid-glide.

'Your first?' The butler strode across to the fireplace. 'Now... open that curtain.'

Footman Steve went over for a press at the switch. Nothing happened. He pressed harder a few times, and suddenly it worked. Suddenly and spectacularly. Open-close/open-close...

'One at a time, one at a time!' Mr Todd was almost shouting. The butler took his curtains seriously.

Five minutes later they were sitting in Mr Todd's pantry. No small-talk, no any kind of talk. Suited Steve, he could think about Alice Kerr.

Finally the butler cleared his throat. 'You say this is your first house party. And when exactly did you commence your training to become a footman?'

Steve's reply was followed by a long, long silence.

Just then the door opened and in walked Alice Kerr carrying a large tray of tea-things – a covered dish, teapot, milk jug, cups and saucers, plates.

She placed it down in front of Mr Todd.

'Very good, Alice. Thank you.'

Steve sat up eagerly, hoping to catch her eye.

Her hair fell slightly forward as she laid everything out on the table, the plates, the cups and saucers. The linen napkin was removed to reveal a stack of sandwiches, real meaty door-stoppers. There was also some fruit. Steve was all ready to give Alice Kerr his friendliest Steve-the-Friendly-Footman smile, but she left without a glance in his direction.

The butler seemed to be retching. 'You'd do better to keep your eyes on the sandwiches, Merrick, you've more chance.' Another retch – this was a laugh, apparently, Todd-style.

After a put-down like that, there was no way Steve was going to say he knew Alice. He'd stick to the roast beef, thick-cut.

His first sandwich bitten, chewed and swallowed down, the butler once again turned his attention to Steve. 'Your accent's from around here.'

'I live in Edinburgh now.'

'Hmm.'

They'd just finished eating when a bell rang.

'The evening begins.' Mr Todd stood up. 'Follow me.'

Classic footman-stance at the bottom of the main stairs. Steve's mouth was dry, his hands trembled; was his waistcoat buttoned properly? His bow-tie clipped straight? He smoothed down his hair for that urbane footman-from-the-city look.

Mr Todd opened the front door.

'Mr Cavendish. Good evening, sir.'

'Ah, Todd.' The guest wore a pinstripe suit and blue tie. 'Good to see you're still here.' Then he turned to the woman beside him, who looked like Britney Spears but even sexier. 'As I was telling you earlier, Christine, Todd is one of the few real gentlemen's gentlemen left in the country.'

The butler's smirk was pure grovel. 'Thank you, sir.'

Mr Todd, Cavendish and Britney Spears made their way upstairs while Steve followed, struggling past the battlefield with a large suitcase in each hand. Then along the corridor.

'The Bangalore Room. Excellent, Todd.'

Cue a grovelling nod from the butler.

Mr Cavendish had the public-school complexion that meant serious money. Britney took off her coat: some parts of her were wearing a very tight-fitting dress.

'Merrick is assigned to you, sir.' Mr Todd motioned him and his suitcases to step forward.

'Over there, I think. The dark blue one.' The man hardly glanced at him.

Steve laid the case over by the dressing-table and stood beside it.

'This is Morton's grandfather, would you believe.' Mr Cavendish crossed the room to show Britney one of the photographs on the wall.

'The jolly old British Empire.' She laughed. 'How very *pukka*!'

Mr Cavendish acknowledged him for the first time. 'Derek, is it?'

'Merrick, sir.'

'Right you are. *Merrick*,' he practised. 'Well, Merrick, could you run me a bath? Not lobster-red. Medium. And you can start unpacking.'

Bath run, lady's suitcase put into her room, gentleman's unpacked, Steve headed down to the main hall. The main hall, by way of the kitchen. Radio babble, the food mixer still whirring. He slowed down as he approached. Eyes right.

Alice Kerr was standing by the sink, wiping the draining board – her back was to him. For several moments he remained in the doorway, watching her. Working out what to say.

He was still trying to decide on his best opening line when Alice turned round and saw him.

'Hello again, Steve.'

Footsteps were coming down the corridor. Mr Todd.

'Alice works better without distractions. And so do you, I'm sure. Mr Wallingham has just arrived. Follow me.'

Steve returned Alice's parting wave, and hurried after the butler.

Steve stood looking on as Mr Todd silently repositioned a nest of Napoleon glasses, one glass at a time, on the dining-table. From the drawing-room next door came the sounds of giggling and *haw-haw* laughter.

It was six minutes to eight. Time for a last nervous dribble followed by a final check that his fly was closed.

He returned to the dining-room. Best footman-stance ready to help the ladies to their seats.

Mr Todd's voice came through the open doorway to the drawing-room:

'Dinner is served.'

Several times during the first course Mr Cavendish indicated the wine bottle, pointed to Britney and ordered Todd to 'Fill her up!' Very flushed under her pale skin, the woman would then make the appropriate engine-noises; the car was getting seriously smashed.

'A good little runner this one.' Cavendish called out. 'Drives well in every gear, especially reverse. Don't you, my sweet.'

She gave an extra loud 'Vroom!' and held out her glass.

The woman opposite Wallingham was dark and gypsy-looking. Playful also: her escort's prawns were being shelled and thrown to her while she tried to catch them in her mouth. Most of the time she missed. She would lean forward, instead, catching them in her cleavage. Purpose-built, it seemed.

Steve could feel himself getting hard. He had to look away, but almost immediately he just had to look back again. Cleavage, cleavage. Cleavage.

He drew in his breath, and held it. His toes curled, his fists clenched, his teeth gritted. He had to think about something else: *the Napoleon glasses, the Bangalore Room, Scottish Clans...*

'I'm getting really hungry, Wally.' The gypsy-looking woman was pleading in such a pathetic little-girl whine that the other gentlemen of the party just *had* to join in to help feed her. Her shoulder strap came down, her cleavage was everywhere.

The Napoleon glasses, Scottish Clans, Scottish Clans, Scottish Clans...

By the end of the meal the car needed directions and some careful handling to make it safely through into the drawing-room.

Afterwards, the butler rinsed and polished the Napoleon glasses while Steve cleared the table and stacked the dishes in the washer. Then he attended to his gentlemen's pyjamas, hung up their travelling clothes, cleaned their bathtubs, put fresh towels on the heated rails, laid out the following day's tweeds and woolly socks.

It was well past midnight when he set off along the corridors and up the uncarpeted stairs looking for his room. No sight of Alice Kerr. Not even in his dreams – he was too exhausted.

7

Next morning Steve took Messrs Wallingham and Cavendish their pre-breakfast tea. At the top of the stairs he came across Britney's evening dress, several yards further, in the middle of the guests' corridor, he found a pair of silk panties. Then a dinner-jacket, a shirt and, all by itself, a single black shoe. A sort of adult paperchase. A few steps later, the second shoe and a pair of trousers. Next to them, a brandy bottle lying on its side.

He knocked on Mr Cavendish's door.

No response.

He knocked again. Then knocked louder.

Still no response.

Even if Mr Cavendish had gone to spend the night with Britney in her own room, the curtains would still have to be opened in his. After one final knock Steve went in.

'Fuck off until you're rung for.' A man's voice came out of the darkness. A woman giggled.

He closed the door. *Pair of bastards.*

He crossed the corridor and knocked on Mr Wallingham's door. Morning tea for two, and no backchat.

On his way out of the library where he'd been seeing to the coffee and newspapers, he met Cavendish-the-bastard.

'Ah, Derek. I was hoping to run into you. When you're bringing the morning tea, a bit later next time, eh?' Gentleman Cavendish smiled, reached forward and stuck something into the front of his waistcoat. 'Good man.' Then he strode off.

Steve took out the crumpled fiver, smoothed it, folded it neatly and stuffed it back in his pocket. The rotten shit hadn't even the decency to place it in his hand, let alone apologise. Soon it would be time to go and see to the fucker's evening clothes, to press them, then lay them out. Laying *him* out would be a lot more appealing…

At lunch the housekeeper sat at the other end of the table, next to a maid called Denise, who probably had a nice personality, and the cook, who certainly hadn't. No Alice Kerr. The women talked among themselves. Mr Todd ate in silence. So did Steve.

The day dragged on. Having set the tea table in the library, seen to the drinks cabinet in the drawing-room, Butler Todd and Footman

Steve began on the dinner table. This took even longer than the previous evening, with the butler down on his hands and knees inspecting the tabletop at eye-level and from every angle as if he was playing snooker. He'd call out instructions: 'The salt a bit more to the left... square up that knife,' and Footman Steve would move the offending item a centimetre across. The jewelled elephant was pirouetted on its ebony base five degrees clockwise as per instruction, several times.

Job finally done, Mr Todd indicated a pile of napkins, told him he wanted mitres and lilies – then walked off.

Steve started work. One fold, the second, a tuck. If he closed his eyes, the linen felt like Alice Kerr's school blouse. He could picture her sitting across from him in Environmental Studies licking the tip of her pencil, her top button undone so that...He was stroking her shoulder now, sliding his arm around her...Her next button was being strained as she breathed in, then out, then in again...

One fold, the second, a tuck. He had to lose his virginity or go completely crazy. Lose it, get rid of it, give it away. He was getting older every minute, getting more obsessed. Whether he was eating, drinking, talking or even folding fucking napkins what was really happening to him was *sex*, or rather the lack of it. He'd go to bed and lie in the dark too stiff to sleep. It burnt him up. Night after night he was in a lather of sweat and hot dreams – his own body-heat turning him over and over, basting him, roasting him. Soon he'd be nothing but a twenty-four-hour hard-on.

Mr Todd returned. He checked the folded napkins: three mitres, three lilies. Four out of the six were failures: one by one they were picked up, shaken out and dropped back onto their place settings. With the butler beside him, Steve mitred and lilied his way once more round the table.

The dining-room had three ceiling-to-floor windows. Outside, beyond the gravel drive and the low stone-urn-topped wall, he could see a lawn that stretched into parkland with, here and there, large oaks and spreading beeches, ending in a line of fir. To the left was the sheen of a small lake complete with a one-tree island. It would be dark soon. For the moment, the wintry sky seemed smoothed to an unblemished pearl-sheen, a flock of geese arced in the distance above the still water – a perfect V-shape pointing to the open moorland beyond. Since his arrival the evening before, Steve hadn't stopped working and hadn't set foot outside, not once. He got more fresh air in the centre of Edinburgh.

Napkins perfect at last, Mr Todd led him to the pantry, opened a large double-doored cupboard stacked with shelf upon shelf of glittering plate, cruet-sets, serving dishes, teapots, coffee pots, milk jugs, cream jugs, sugar bowls, at least half a dozen pairs of sugar tongs, plus an armoury of dinner forks, dessert forks, spoons, teaspoons, serving spoons, soup spoons, ladles, dinner knives, cake knives, butter knives…Everything was slotted into its own compartment in layers of green felt-lined drawers, or else placed on shelves and arranged according to size and purpose.

'The silver,' announced Mr Todd.

'Very nice.'

Mr Todd handed him a fluffy yellow cloth, a tin of polish, told him to get busy, and left.

For a moment Steve was tempted to call after him, asking if this particular task came under his job description. Wasn't the butler simply taking the opportunity to delegate one of his own weekly chores? But, apart from Todd himself, who was there to appeal to?

Steve picked out the smallest object he could see, an egg cup. He glared at it. A solid silver egg cup, for fuck's sake, and seven more waiting their turn. He cursed it, then began polishing. Four egg cups later he paused for a long blank stare out the window…

'Rest time?' Alice Kerr was standing in the doorway.

'Now that you're here, it is.'

For the next few minutes they talked about his leaving school, getting a job, about the agency townhouse in Edinburgh and – with a few embellishments – Steve's new life in the big city. She told him that Mr Todd was her grandfather and that sometimes when there were guests at the weekend, she helped out. She asked if he had a girlfriend. He gave the nearest egg cup a few flicks with his yellow cloth, and tried to look city-wise.

She asked, 'So you don't fancy me any more?'

'Who said that I—?'

'Your pal Billy. He told Kirsty.'

'But I never said he was to—'

'Everybody knew anyway!' She laughed. 'So, got a girlfriend in Edinburgh, have you?'

'Well, when you're in the city, there's parties every night and—'

'So I'm asking, Steve – you don't fancy me anymore?'

'No – I mean, well...'

'Well?'

'Aye.'

'Aye?'

'Aye, I still fancy you.'

'Like to kiss me, would you, Steve?'

'Oh...Aye.'

'You don't sound that sure.'

'Oh, I am. I really am...sure.'

'Well then...?'

'Well...' He took a step towards her. He stood facing her. He thought: I am going to kiss Alice Kerr. To kiss *Alice Kerr*.

She picked up the egg cup he'd just polished. She breathed on it, then buffed it on the sleeve of her blouse. 'So I'll have to think whether to let you or not. After all...' She inspected the newly shone egg cup, then replaced it in the sideboard. 'After all, you'll soon be going straight back up to Edinburgh, straight out of my life.'

'Not till tomorrow.'

'Far in the future as that, eh? Real long-term commitment. I'll need to have a think to myself.' She paused, 'You look cute, mind, in the bow-tie and all.' Then she left.

Steve grabbed the next egg cup and began polishing.

That evening, while tucking into their sandwiches, Mr Todd started swilling down wine like he wanted to drown in the stuff. When the time came for serving dinner he set a bottle and glass just inside the pantry and helped himself as he passed to and from the dining-room.

Only when dinner was finished and the two of them were standing in the pantry did Steve realise how drunk Mr Todd was. The butler made a slurred announcement to the effect that the Napoleon glasses wouldn't be touched till the morning. 'The voice of bitter experience,' came the explanation. Steve was invited to sit down. Some wine was poured for him.

Mr Todd raised his own glass and gave a drunken grin.

'Cheers, Steven!'

Steven? They drank.

'You've done not bad, son. Still got a lot to learn, of course.'

Real praise, Scottish-style.

Mr Todd carried on, 'Not that *they'd* notice. Hardly even see the person they're throwing their food at, let alone acknowledge a servant.' He filled up Steve's glass, and refilled his own. They drank. There was a pause that lasted well over a minute.

'My grandfather started here as second silver-boy.' The butler slurred his way across the words. 'That was when there were three hall-boys, four footmen, a valet and the butler. Only inside the house, mind. Outside – a head gardener, under-gardener, labourers, head groom…So many. So many. Silver-boy, hall-boy, footman, valet, butler. Second silver-boy, then first silver-boy, then third hall-boy, fourth footman, you follow me?'

'Yes.' Steve was very tired.

'It took years, was a career. My grandfather became butler, was respected by everyone. Everyone. Then my father, as well.' He poured more wine. 'Those days, the butler lived better than the master. Didn't lift a finger, had all the staff he wanted. Something needed done? My grandfather just nodded the slightest nod...' Mr Todd lolled heavily to one side in illustration, 'and one of the footmen would jump to it. Jump to it!' More wine. 'In the village my grandfather was the man they all wanted to know.' He drew himself up very straight. 'Into the local and they'd be clamouring to buy him a drink, queuing up. He'd the say-so for any jobs on the estate. The master was the master, but he was the *boss*!' Mr Todd all but shouted the word *boss,* and slammed the palm of his hand down on the table. He leant across, tried to focus. And failed.

'I'm telling you, Steven. God's truth.'

Another long pause, then the butler continued. 'A good weekend's work. You gave us no short measures and we'll give you none.' This time he overfilled Steve's glass. 'Thy cup runneth over.' Then emptied his own, and refilled it.

'Silver-boy, hall-boy, footman, valet, then butler. So, so many. You with me? But who cares now? No staff. I have to set the table myself, iron the clothes and even drive the bloody car. In the town they think I'm some kind of domesticated *waiter*.' He spat out the word. 'And what happens when I retire? Well, Steven, I'll tell you. I should be retired now, but I've no house. It's tied.'

Another pause.

'They say the whole set-up's coming round again. So *they* say...the Cavendishes and the Wallinghams of this new Scotland. The rich getting richer, the poor getting poorer. More masters and more servants. Christ, if the good times are coming to this country, I hope they come pretty damn soon. Or I'll be out on my ear and sleeping in the streets unless I'm lucky enough to drop dead on the job.'

Mr Todd drank off the rest of his wine in one swallow, and poured out more.

'What I say, Steven, is: fuck the lot of them. The captains of industry and their weekend tarts, the lords, the dukes – getting pensioned off now but they'll be bobbing back up again before you know it. Them, or something much like it. I'd like to show them out like a good butler should. Show them the door? – I'd show them the fucking gangplank! Captains of industry, they call themselves! Renaming the ship'll no save them! Don't they know the fucking ship's sinking?'

Steve nodded. He was almost asleep.

'A toast.' Mr Todd hauled himself to his feet, his left hand clutching the table edge to keep steady, and raised his glass:

'To the rest of us, not the sinking rats but those still on board; the crew, that is — not the bloody passengers!' He emptied his glass. 'G'night.' Then lurched out of the kitchen.

Mr Todd's dramatic exit was spoiled thirty seconds later when he stuck his head back in the door.

'Alice is my granddaughter, y'know. Nice lass. Might be housekeeper one day.' He gave a big wink, then staggered off out of the room.

The following morning Steve was folding up his footman uniform, tucking up the tails to fit into his suitcase, when there was a light knock at his bedroom door.

It was Alice. Alice Kerr the big tease.

'Grandfather says he'll take you the station – be ready to leave in ten minutes.'

'Thanks.' He carried on packing.

'So I've come to say goodbye and wish you all the best in the big city.'

'Right. Thanks.'

All those stories – she'd probably never been with anyone at all, let alone two at the same time. Anyway, what did he care? Plenty more in Edinburgh. He shoved the tails in anyhow, scrunched up the trousers, rammed them in on top and closed the lid with a snap.

Alice was still speaking. 'One thing I nearly forgot.'

And before Steve realised what was happening, Alice Kerr had stepped forward, put her hands on his shoulders and kissed him.

She stepped back again. 'Very best of luck, Steve – and let's keep in touch, eh!' She pressed a piece of paper into his hand. 'Here's my mobile number.' Then she gave him a big smile – he managed an inane grin in return. Next moment, she was gone.

Steve stood quite still for several moments, hardly able to breathe: Alice Kerr had actually kissed him. Alice...Kerr.

Alice. Alice. He whispered her name over and over. Alice had walked towards him, Alice had placed her hands on his shoulders and kissed him. Alice had given him her number and said she wanted him to call her. This, he suddenly knew, was the moment when his real life began. Not when he'd walked out of school, not when he'd left home, not when he'd found a job – but *now*!

'Yes,' he cried out loud to the empty room, then to the whole of Craigbar House, to the lawn, the woods and fields, the whole countryside and the world beyond. 'YES! YES! YES!'

He had to hurry the rest of his packing. In his excitement he kept forgetting things. He opened and closed the suitcase several times – for the toiletries, for the footman shoes, for the collar studs and cufflinks. Finally he snapped it shut and locked it.

Then unlocked and opened it again. His pyjamas.

He rushed downstairs. A shiny black, four-wheel-drive SUV was waiting for him at the back door, a rather hungover-looking Mr. Todd at the wheel.

Just before they drove out of the courtyard Steve glanced back, hoping to catch sight of Alice at a window, perhaps, or standing in the doorway, waving him goodbye. But they turned the corner of the house too quickly.

First thing back in Edinburgh he'd buy himself a new mobile and call her. All that about her and older men, and her being easy, all that nonsense – that complete and utter fucking nonsense. Of course it wasn't true. And now he was glad. He was so very, very glad.

Fiction
Crime
Noir

Culture
Music
Erotica

dare to read at serpentstail.com

Visit serpentstail.com today to browse and buy
our books, and to sign up for exclusive news and
previews of our books, interviews with our
authors and forthcoming events.

NEWS — cut to the literary chase with all the latest news about our books and authors

EVENTS — advance information on forthcoming events, author readings, exhibitions and book festivals

EXTRACTS — read the best of the outlaw voices – first chapters, short stories, bite-sized extracts

EXCLUSIVES — pre-publication offers, signed copies, discounted books, competitions

BROWSE AND BUY — browse our full catalogue, fill up a basket and proceed to our fully secure checkout – our website is your oyster

FREE POSTAGE & PACKING ON ALL ORDERS…
ANYWHERE!

---

sign up today – join our club